No part of this publication may be reproduced, stored in a retrieval system, or transmitted in any form or by any means, electronic, mechanical, photocopying, recording, scanning, or otherwise, without the prior written permission of the publisher, except in the case of brief quotations within critical reviews and otherwise as permitted by copyright law.

NOTE: This is a work of fiction. Names, characters, places, and incidents are a product of the author's imagination. Any resemblance to real life is purely coincidental. All characters in this story are 18 or older.

Copyright © 2019, Willow Winters Publishing. All rights reserved.

Madox & Sophie

Willow Winters
Wall street journal & usa today bestselling author

From USA Today bestselling author, Willow Winters, comes a seductive and emotionally captivating second-chance romance.

It's impossible to get over what we had.
He was everything — irresistibly handsome, ruthlessly elite, and seemingly untouchable — while I was nothing.
Yet he protected me when I was at my lowest;
more than that, he wanted me.

He devoured me... and I did the same to him.
Until it all fell apart
and I ran as far away from Madox as I could.
After all, the two of us were never meant to be together.

I never thought I'd see him again, years later. Let alone be under him in the way I've craved since we said goodbye.

The attraction between us still burns like fire, but time can't change the past. And I don't know if it's possible for us to mend all of our broken pieces.

Tell Me
To Stay

Seven years ago

"Why do you keep looking at me like that?" I ask him from across the room. A room far too large for what it is. I'm not used to houses like this.

"Like what?"

"Like you can't look anywhere else." I can feel my cheeks burning from knowing he's watching me as I read. My response is meant to sound exasperated and maybe frustrated. Instead, my words are breathless and vulnerability lingers in every syllable.

"Your answer is in your question, Soph."

Prologue

Maddox

I didn't know she'd left me until her plane had already taken off. That's the shittiest part of it.

We fucked. We fought. We shared every part of our flawed pieces with each other. That's the way it always was with us. Apparently, that wasn't enough to keep her that night.

I didn't get another word from her after the "fuck you" she spat at me right before her front door slammed in my face. No matter how hard I banged on her apartment door, demanding an answer for why she'd done what she did. I can still feel the way the anger rolled off me as I stood there in the hall for far too long, wondering what the fuck I was even doing there. I didn't belong in her world — just like she didn't belong in mine. Shit, my Armani suit didn't need to spend a single second on that side of the bridge.

But I'd followed her there just the same. That's what she did to me. We broke each other down to the raw bits that only acted on primal needs. Fighting and fucking. No one ever made me lose it like she did. No one ever made me feel as high, as needed... or as loved as she did, either.

Seeing her across the bar three years later does something to me I've never felt before. As I lift the whiskey to my lips, the ice clinks against the glass as the music fades to white noise. All I can see is the way her lips stay parted ever so slightly after she takes a sip of her drink.

It's like slow motion.

All I can hear is the hum of satisfaction I know is about to slip from those pouty lips the second her glass hits the bar top.

She came back.

All I can feel is my cock getting harder by the second.

And I need her to love me just as much as I need to punish her for leaving me the way she did.

Chapter 1

Sophie
Seven Years Ago

"I didn't think I scared you," he says and Madox's voice is rough until he clears his throat.

"You don't," I answer him although my heart beats wildly inside of me, as if slamming against my rib cage in denial of what I just said.

"Then why do you keep looking at me like that?"

"Like what?"

His smirk is slow to form. It's wicked and charming, just like Madox himself.

"Like you're waiting for me to pounce on you."

With a slight tilt of my head and my blood pressure rising, I simply give Madox words he's told me before. "Your answer is in your question."

Today

There's something about flying that makes me horny. Not full blown, not like that. Just… turned on a little. Like a smidgen.

Maybe it's fear; the perceived danger, even though I know logically it's the safest way to travel. Still, as the engine rumbles and roars in my ears, I feel the vibrations intensify under me. My eyes close, my breathing hitches, and I have to grip the edge of the seat.

Pathetic, aren't you? Is your life really that boring? My inner voice is a bitch, but she's not wrong.

The snide thought makes me smirk, even while my heart lurches as the plane finally leaves the safety of land. I almost laugh at my ridiculous response. Especially given I'm in the close confines of coach seating with so many strangers, all of us headed from San Francisco to New York.

It's a long flight to sit this close to someone. I peek up after feeling the rush, offering a polite and tight-lipped smile to the elderly lady on my right, in the middle seat. The woman and the man next to her in the aisle seat, who I assume is her husband, are already preparing their neck pillows to nap and neither of them pays me any attention.

Thank God.

Leaning closer to the window to glance out, placing most of my weight on the armrest, I let the relief wash through me as my heartbeat slows back down.

Time ticks by, the droning sound of the pilot speaking muffled by the white noise of the plane, and as the plane settles, so does that feeling deep in my belly.

My grip goes from white knuckled to loose, and my pulse returns to normal. The jitters that hit me for a brief moment, that tiny moment when I questioned if I would be all right, those jitters eventually subside. The desire fades too.

It's not always like this.

I know part of the reason I feel this way is because I'm going back to *his* city. The hints of apprehension and thoughts of him make for a deadly concoction.

It's odd to think of New York as if it's dominated by a single man. But he's the only one who's always ruled it as far as I'm concerned. Even when we were teenagers.

Madox Reed takes what he wants; he always has. Irresistibly handsome, ruthlessly elite, and seemingly untouchable, there was nothing that he couldn't have back then. And so New York simply belongs to him in my eyes. Even if it's an utterly ridiculous thought.

I wish he'd stay in the past where he belongs. It's fucking killing me that I'm letting the thoughts of a man I once knew bother me so damn much.

I cross and uncross my legs, pretending like he doesn't

matter and as if this anxiety I'm feeling is solely because I'm flying. I've always been shitty at lying to myself though. Yeah, these nerves aren't from the plane, they're because of him.

He's been on my mind ever since I packed my final bag last night. If I'm honest with myself, ever since the phone call saying I got the job and learned I'd be moving back to New York, I've been thinking of him. But this has to stop. This is about new beginnings and my past will stay right there, where it belongs. In the past.

Trisha's dropping off my boxes at the post office today and with those last three shipped, everything I own will be delivered to 55 Thompson Street, apartment 617 in gorgeous SoHo. I owe her more than a few drinks when she finally comes to visit me. I hope she comes sooner rather than later.

I'll be alone in the city, and my one friend is all the way across the country now.

Trish's brother, Brett, is technically a friend as well, and he's always been kind to me. He's also technically in New York but friends with Madox, so there's no fucking way I'll be contacting him. None of those guys will be getting a message from me to let them know I'm back. No. Fucking. Way.

They were a tight crew back then and I know Brett, or any of the guys for that matter, would tell Madox I've returned. So that shit's not happening. No matter how much I miss everyone. I left our entire group of friends – basically my family — and I up and left without a word, tagging along with Trish.

A heavy exhale leaves me slowly as I watch the clouds surround us.

I don't even want to think about them. So yeah, I won't be reaching out to any of them, but if worse comes to worst, I know Brett would be there for me. He's a last resort.

At the thought of what I left years ago – and why – the knots in my stomach tighten and I have to readjust in my seat, pulling out the magazine I bought during my two-hour wait at the terminal.

I'd rather think about Madox and all the dirty shit he did to me than what his group of friends – my *former* friends – will think of me coming back.

The plane dips and so does my stomach, as if it's some sign to stop thinking about him, but in true fashion, it only causes a blush to rise to my cheeks. When all's said and done, I'm left feeling like I'm hiding a secret from however many people are on this plane, holding a wrinkled issue of the most recent edition of *Elle Décor* in my hands.

Oops.

I take a minute to smooth it out, trying to pull myself together. *Soon I'll be able to afford something in these glossy pages.*

The clouds stream past on the other side of the cool window and I watch until they're beneath us and we're riding in nothing but a vibrant hue of blue.

It's better for me that I take this position, even if it is in New York. I don't know how many times I've told myself that. It's best that I work for a company with an established background and steady clients lined up. I'm damn good at what I do, and things are finally going my way.

I know how to turn failing businesses around and I can spot an error in marketing faster than a new bakery can post to Instagram with a rookie mistake – perfectly decorated cupcakes, plus a sink full of dirty dishes in the background. Love is in the details, and I know every damn detail that matters.

But I'm young for the industry, in my mid-twenties. San Francisco was … expensive. Bills added up and I'm ashamed that I couldn't afford it all myself. I took a risk investing everything that I had into myself, my brand, my company.

I have to swallow hard after the next breath. Pride is a lumpy fucker. I was going to let Trish keep bailing me out and covering my half of the rent. But this is a stable job with no risk. It's where I could hope to be ten years from now on my own. This job is a blessing, even if it's coming after falling a little short on my own.

I'd do it all over again if I could. I'll always invest in myself and my passions. Even if I had to work for free just to fill out a résumé. That's where I went wrong, I think. I felt bad for people I knew could succeed if only their branding were more to market, if only they invested in advertising, if only they managed their social media better… if only, if only, if only. If only I'd charged them what I should have, instead of going above and beyond, all while working pro bono.

At least word got around that I'm good at what I do. *It was worth it.* For a position as a branding advisor in Candor Designs, the most sought-after marketing firm in the country.

It was worth it, and everything happens for a reason. I may not have made money, but I made a damn good name for myself.

As I'm toeing my satchel back under the seat in front of me, I barely look up and catch the flight attendant telling me about the drink cart and how only cards are accepted. The smile on my face is a genuine response. I open the magazine pretending I'm not still thinking about my first love and how every minute that passes, I'm getting that much closer to him.

Our memories are what make us who we are. The majority of mine from when I grew up are consumed with Madox, although I've been able to avoid them since I moved away. Most of the time, anyway.

That giddiness, that fear I felt only moments ago when the plane took off is familiar to me. It's the same thing I feel when I think of Madox. Every time. I've never stopped loving him, but sometimes fate simply doesn't let love be enough.

I'm not going to spend the entire flight thinking about him. I'm starting over, not looking back. My resolve is firm as I turn the pages of the magazine.

I just hope I don't see him again. After all, New York is filled with so many people. And there's only one of him. Even if he rules the city.

CHAPTER 2

SOPHIE
SEVEN YEARS AGO

It's different when there's no one else with us. Last week I didn't want anyone else around, but now? The thought of being alone with him makes my skin heat with a fire I've never felt before.

"Hey." Madox nudges my elbow with his as he leans in closer and asks me, "You want to get out of here?"

The thumpity-thump inside my chest can't be ignored. It's so loud I'm sure everyone in here can hear it.

"Where do you want to go?" I ask him, knowing that even before he gives me an answer, "yes" is already waiting to slip past my lips.

"Name it," he tells me like that it's that easy. "We can go wherever you want."

Alone. Is there a place called Alone? *Somewhere we can be by ourselves.*

I want to see what this fire turns into when he touches me.

TODAY

I'm here.

I text Trish the second I finally make it to Thompson Street. My phone instantly buzzes with a response and then another as I gaze out the front window of my brand-spanking-new apartment and then look back to the expansive dining room. I feel sick and anxious. None of this is me. It feels too expensive, too chic.

Too much like how it felt when I realized what the other side of this world is like when I first met Maddox ... *and there I go thinking of him again.*

Too much like a woman trying to fit into a world that doesn't belong to her. From the thick silk curtains lining the floor-to-ceiling windows that could have come straight from that *Elle Décor* magazine, to the accent pillows that would be stained with makeup if I dared lay my head on them.

There's too much white. Too many hard lines.

Too much money being spent on me that I didn't earn... *Yet.*

My finger hovers over the send button. I'm struggling

to compose a message to Adrienne, the woman who hired me and told me this place was covered by my employer. No matter how many times I read the text I wrote, rewrite it and read it again, I sound like an ungrateful bitch.

Dammit! I roll my eyes as I delete it, warring with how I want to handle this situation. I should roll with the punches, get my footing, prove my worth and then take charge.

It really is too much though. I can't believe a company would give all this to me when I haven't even worked a single day yet.

My cardboard moving boxes, filled with IKEA merchandise, don't belong here.

I take another slow walk around the first floor and a faster one upstairs. The apartment's ready to live in. Even the fridge already contains milk and eggs. When I first got to the address, I thought I must have been mistaken. Although the key fit, it was obviously someone else's house. But the parchment on the dining room table read: *Welcome Sophie, make yourself at home. We start on Monday.*

Signed by the one and only Adrienne Hart.

The tips of my fingers are numb as I shove my phone into a wristlet. The sky is gray and rain is most certainly looming, so I dig through three boxes marked "closet" until I find one with a hoodie in it and head straight for the door.

I didn't earn this. It makes me feel like I've missed something or the expectations they have for me are higher than I anticipated. *Maybe this is what having Imposter syndrome feels like.*

Trish has already called three times, so I call her as I head downtown, searching for a place to eat or grab a drink. I look like shit; feel like it too. But this is New York. You can look like whatever you want here, and as long as you can pay the bill, no one gives a shit.

As the phone rings, I start thinking more about drinks and less about food.

Because that's what I really need, a giant chill pill at the bottom of a martini glass.

"You're freaking out," Trish tells me the second I say hi.

"Yeah." I breathe out the word, feeling the energy of the fast-paced city move around me. It's dark, getting darker by the second and it's true what they say; the city comes to life at night.

"What's going on?" Trish asks and I can hear another question lingering, but she doesn't voice it completely. With cars beeping and everyone else on their phone all around me, it's hectic, but I love it. In this city, it's easy to blend in. A person can get lost here in the crowds.

I like fading into the background. I prefer to go unnoticed.

"It just seems like so much pressure, or..." I pause, making a left as I quicken my pace so I can cross before the green man on the crosswalk sign changes to a bright red hand. "It just happened really quickly and it seems like too much."

"You don't think you're worth it." Trish's voice carries through the phone with equal amounts of hardness and insight.

I almost stop in the middle of the street, even as the green man symbol starts to flash, a warning that the mean red hand is coming.

"You *are* worth it. If you can find someone willing to pay you an obscene amount of money to do what you love, you're worth *that* amount. Period." Trish's self-assurance comes from a different upbringing than mine. She lived here too, three years ago. Two different family lives though. I imagine Trish could have grown up on these very streets.

The posh shops and chic cafes with macarons would have been her favorite shops at only five years old when she wore lace and learned how to behave in boarding school.

She and Brett would have ruled these streets. Thinking about Brett makes me smile. Being the younger of the two of them, he got away with bloody murder and loved how it riled her up. He's a goofball who can also fit in with high society.

Trish *is* high society. She is whatever she wants to be.

She was salutatorian in her high school, and she graduated with a double degree by the time she was twenty-four. She wanted to leave NYC and make a name for herself as an artist in San Francisco. When I asked her if I could come with her, I wasn't sure what she'd say. It was last minute and I wasn't in the best of places back then. We weren't particularly close either. I was just one of her brother's friend's ex-girlfriends – sort of, not even an ex really – she'd seen me come and go throughout the years. But I was also someone in desperate need that night to get away from here and everything else. The same night I left Madox.

Oh, how things have changed.

"Hey, turn right, right here." Trish's tone changes and her words catch me off guard.

"Are you tracking me?" My voice reflects the ridiculousness of the situation. "When I gave you permission to see my location it was to help me when I get lost... Not to track me like a stalker," I joke with her and she only laughs. I'm prone to getting lost. In life and on city streets both. My inner bitch shrugs and keeps filing her nails.

"Trust me, there's a bar right around the corner I've heard good things about. Are you wearing something cute?"

I glance down at my hoodie and lie, "Yes."

"You are so full of shit." I can only laugh as she tells me, "When you look good, you feel good."

Staring at the bright lights to a bar called The Tipsy Room, I breathe in deep, feeling her confidence. "I see it," I tell her, although she probably already knows because of her app. "You can turn that thing off now, you creeper."

"After one drink, you'll be thanking me," she jokes back.

"You should really quit your day job and do self-empowerment classes, you know?" I tease and let the people around me pass me by quickly as I take my time heading to the bar.

"I'd rather keep mine, thank you very much." As she answers,

I can practically hear the smile in her voice. "And as for you, this job and that apartment – you earned those. Be proud."

The anxiety is still there deep inside of me as I think about my cardboard boxes sitting in the middle of the gorgeous hand-tufted rug in the living room. "It's just a lot."

"Well, you're worth a lot... and New York is 'a lot.' You know that." I can hear myself swallow as I nod, even though she can't see.

"I'm going to get a drink."

Before I can tell her I'll call her when I get back to my new home, she's already commanding me to do just that in her motherly voice. I'm telling her I love her back as I walk into the place frowning down at my attire, but too tired from the plane ride and stressed from the move to give a fuck.

It takes about two whole seconds for me to realize The Tipsy Room is going to be my go-to place for the rest of eternity. Black chandeliers hang from the ceilings, which are at least ten feet high, and the lights are dimmed to the point where it feels cozy, but bright enough to see all the fine details in the rugged wood tables. Cast iron chairs and barstools with a slick granite bar top give the place a sense of coldness. And a white quartz fireplace in the very center of the space with ottomans surrounding it give the décor the warmth it needs.

Whoever designed this place has my entire approval. The music is soft, yet upbeat. And it smells like a cool drink on a seaside beach. I'm in love with this place.

New York may hit me like a brick in my stomach every time I come here, but I'm calling tonight a win already.

Climbing onto a barstool at the very back, I immediately grab a thick paper menu and listen to the quiet chatter from the half-full bar and a roar of laughter from somewhere on my left.

As my eyes spot the very drink I know I'd love to order day in and day out – a combination of grapefruit and tequila – my heart skips a beat. Or at least I think it's skipped one, but then it doesn't beat at all.

Not until the laughter dies, and I tell myself there's no fucking way it's him. My face is instantly hot and my hands are clammy. I keep repeating to myself that I'm a fool, it's not him, it only sounded like the memories of my past because I'm hung up on Madox.

But then I hear it again, the familiar roughness of it. The deep cadence of his chuckle somehow standing out in the bar. Even though my body is instinctively still, like a child hiding in the closet, I glance to my left and see a room off the side of the bar. Judging by the size, it's probably for parties.

I can't see him. No.

But my throat gets tight as I see some friends who I used to love. *His* friends really, but once upon a time they were my friends. Trish's brother, Brett, is within view. His sweet but sarcastic voice is carrying on with some story as he runs his hand through his shaggy hair.

I can't make out what he's saying; everything turns to

white noise except for the loud ringing in my ears telling me to get the fuck out. The barstool nearly tips over as I push away from the counter, ignoring a bartender who happens to walk up the second I'm tumbling out of the high seat.

Don't look.

I can barely fucking breathe. With my head down and my cheeks hot, my legs move numbly. All the memories come flooding back at once, but I'm distracted with the anxiousness churning in my gut.

What are the fucking odds?

Shit, shit, shit. I'm going on nearly twenty-four hours without sleep and dressed in a rumpled hoodie with day-old mascara.

I could kill someone right now. *Trisha.* I mouth her name like a curse. She set me up! There's no way she didn't know Brett was here. I tell myself it was only Brett she knew about and not Madox. She wouldn't do that to me. There's no way she could have known he was here.

Unless Brett told her. Unless she wanted me to get back together with Madox. Which isn't at all like her. Staring blankly at the bottles of wine on the back wall, I know there's no way Trisha would have sent me here knowing Madox was here; she knows how much it all still hurts to think about.

She could have given me a heads-up at least if she knew Brett was going to be around.

Madox is here. I text her and watch the bubble form letting me know she's texting back.

Holy shit! Did he see you?

Not yet.

What are you going to do? she asks and I at least feel relief at knowing she didn't plan this. She didn't set me up to run into him tonight.

Before I can answer she texts me, *I'm sorry! Brett said it was a good bar – I didn't know Madox would be there – I swear!*

If I thought I was freaking out before I got to the bar, I thought wrong. This is a real reason to have a damn panic attack. I didn't even make it four hours in the city before running into Madox again. Fate is a cruel bitch. She can go fuck herself.

Madox Reed is only about two dozen feet away from me, and although he's tucked away in a side room of this bar, I cannot bring myself to face him right now.

The last time I saw him, he took me the way he always fucked me back then.

Ruthlessly, and with an unforgiving passion that left me breathless. In a back alley behind a bar, no less. After I left, he came to my place, hunting me down. Those are the last memories he has of me.

There's no way I can face him right now.

I barely manage to hide behind the brick of the fireplace, not that I'm sure he's even aware of my existence right now. I let myself breathe for a second, shaking out my hands and giving the small gathering of girls to my left a small smile when they look my way.

I have to pretend I'm not thinking of that night. And that I'm not freaking the fuck out.

What are the odds?

I can feel every single second of what happened that last night.

I remember how my nails scratched down his back and my shoulders hit the hood of the car; I remember how I let my neck arch, breaking our kiss so I could breathe.

With his lips roaming down my neck and his teeth grazing along my sensitized skin, my heart hammered and pleasure built deep in the pit of my stomach. I feel it all over again as I lean against the brick wall to keep me steady.

Even though we hadn't talked since our last fight – we did that often back then – getting into fights where I walked away, and we didn't see each other for a while. Not unless I went back to him. Which I always did. That night in particular, I missed him. Everything was wrong, and I had no one.

I craved the way he looked at me with nothing but hunger in his dark green eyes.

And I needed someone. Desperately.

That night I was suffering, and I knew he could take the pain away.

Even now I can admit I wanted him to fuck me because it felt like nothing else mattered when I shattered beneath him. When I let him use me how he liked, savagely and with reckless abandon.

Even if we were nothing other than lovers in that moment. He never called me his girlfriend, he never gave me a commitment. Never. That night, I needed to go far away and I knew he could take me there.

I fell back into his arms without second-guessing a damn thing, and the next thing I knew, I was staring off into the distance while he savagely fucked me in a back alley.

I felt the rush of pleasure as he groaned in the crook of my neck, but it was met with a pain that twisted my heart.

When he nipped at my ear, he called me his dirty whore and ecstasy rocked deep inside of me with his words. He told me I was his to fuck and use how he wanted, and I loved it. In that moment, I loved every bit of it.

He told me to cum for him, and I did. I came with him, like so many times before. I unraveled underneath of him. But what was left of me when he was done was something I didn't want to face.

When it was over, and the reality of what had happened left me cold and hating myself for what I'd allowed.

Just as I need to run now, I ran back then. As fast and far away as I could. I ran back to my apartment and called Trish because I knew she was moving across the country, and I wanted to go too. I needed to leave after everything that had happened that week. Madox didn't know any of it. I didn't tell him anything that happened and so much had that week, but it didn't matter. I didn't tell him anything, because he never told me anything either. It was sex. That's all we had by the end. I knew I needed to leave. And she said yes, I could come with her.

Facing Madox after leaving him the way I did... I can't fucking do it now.

I sought him out, fucked him – I used him the way he used me. Instead of going back inside the bar to hang out with everyone afterward, like we always did, I ran.

I didn't know he'd come after me when he figured out I didn't go back to the bar. When he showed up at my apartment, I pushed him away and said everything I could to make him leave. Rather than telling him what had happened and why I cried myself to sleep every night that week. He never gave me a commitment. He never gave me a reason to stay. He'd never come after me before and only did that night because he was angry I'd left without telling him. I don't know what he expected from me, but I ruined it all.

It was my fault. Everything that night was my fault. I never should have gone to him.

That's the last time I spoke to Madox Reed, three years ago. Other than a single text I sent the next morning.

With a blink, the memory fades and the bar seems even more vibrant and lively as I round the corner – not even getting to order my drink, dammit – and search for the exit. *I need to get out of here.*

"Sorry." The word slips from me as I accidentally brush against someone walking by and she spills her drink.

"Shit," she says, and the girl just laughs it off, her blonde hair tumbling down her back as she dabs at her arm with a pale blue cocktail napkin. The smile on her face only broadens, and she leans into another woman who apologizes to me as if it was her friend's fault.

The second girl's smile dims as I merely stare back at them, not coming up with any words. *Snap out of it.*

I need to get the hell out of here.

Swallowing thickly, I turn and head for the door. So close. So close to getting away from him and never setting foot back in this place – or even on this street – it's blacklisted now.

The second I open the door to the bar, the rain spills down, and Ryan Jacobs of all people is right fucking there. Madox's best friend – *shit, don't see me.*

I stop and stand awkwardly outside of the bar like a deer caught in headlights – *don't see me*. The street, which is constantly busy, is fucking empty as I stand on the two feet of sidewalk protected by the awning. Of course it is. Leaving me nowhere to hide, and only Ryan to gawk at. He looks me right in the eye, blowing smoke from his cigarette before letting his lips tip up into a smile. He looks older than when I last saw him, but age looks damn good on him. His leather jacket creases around his shoulders as he stubs out his cig, carelessly flicking it to the side before heading straight for me.

It's a good thing I'm not an undercover cop or on the run from the mafia. I apparently suck at hiding in plain sight.

"Hey." The word crawls from me, hanging in the air as I try to form a smile that matches the genuine grin on his stubbled face.

"I can't believe my eyes," Ryan tells me before wrapping his arms around me and giving me a hug I've missed so much. And what can I do?

They were my family. My friends.

When I left Madox, I left everyone.

He holds me tighter when I squeeze him back. And that's when Brett walks out behind us, giving me the widest smile.

Fuck me. Fuck New York. Fuck this damn bar.

"I can't believe you're back, baby girl."

Baby girl. They all called me that for the longest time. I had to ask Trisha to stop when she let it slip a few times the first week after we'd moved. I told her everything and how much it hurt. These guys though? I don't know what they know. I never told them anything. Apparently I'm still *baby girl* to them though, and selfishly, that makes me happy.

"We need to celebrate with a drink," Ryan says and starts pulling me toward the door. My heels dig in to the ground and I hesitate, my resolve to stay far away from Madox still firm. Until both Brett and Ryan look back at me, the questions in their eyes mixed with a touch of shock and pain.

It's gone quickly, but it was there.

"Madox is in there," I point out and wonder if they'll lie to get me inside. "I don't... I haven't..." I don't bother finishing, since every start to the sentence leaves me feeling childish.

"It's been a long time," Ryan says after a while and then shoves his hands in his jacket pockets. "We don't have to invite him over for drinks," he offers, as if Madox ever asked for an invitation.

"Come on Soph, don't do us like that. We miss you," Brett tells me and opens the door a little wider. "I promise you the drinks are good and the first one's on me."

I could never turn down Brett. It was weird seeing him the first time at Trish's in San Francisco, but only until he hugged me. He's a guy who's hard not to love.

"Just one drink?" Ryan asks in his charming puppy-dog voice he knows gets me every time and I cave. The two of them are too damn sweet and too damn cute to say no to. And I owe them. I owe them both more than I can ever repay them.

"Just one." They both cheer and wrap an arm around me, ushering me in the second I agree. As though I'll change my mind and bolt if they don't get me to the bar as quick as they can.

I know Madox is going to find out I'm here in T-minus five seconds. If by some miracle he doesn't see me tonight, then they'll tell him. Deep in my gut, I know I'm kidding myself to think he's not going to be right at the bar beside me in just a moment.

I brace myself for the inevitable.

As I follow Brett and Ryan, smiling and laughing as they head to the bar and announce to the bartender their good friend is back in town, I think, *what the fuck happened to keeping the past in the past?*

Chapter 3

Madox
Seven Years Ago

"So you and Sophie?" Ryan asks me and I look him up and down as he stands in the doorway. I don't know what to tell him, or the other guys... It just happened.

"I didn't think you'd go for it," he adds when I don't answer him right away.

"Why's that?" I ask him and he tilts his head to the left, as if to say, 'you already know.'

"Yeah," I tell him, thinking about how we hooked up last night and the night before and how much I wanted her this morning, even knowing I shouldn't have touched her in the first place. "Me and Sophie."

"You know what people will say, right?" he asks and that's when I tell him to fuck off.

Today

Long days at the office.

Long nights at this bar. *My* bar.

I've spent a lot of nights sitting back and wondering what she'd think about it.

Which is why this moment doesn't feel real. I'm only a shot and one beer in; I don't even feel a buzz. However, for a split second, I question whether or not I'm just seeing what I want to see.

I only got up to check on the bartenders and the inventory. Standing at the far end, I see the one girl I've been waiting to see for so long.

"Whiskey," I order the second I see Samantha, one of the waitresses, walking by me, headed to the back. My eyes don't move to her to see if she's heard me or not. I can't rip them away from the girl at the bar.

Two and a half years I shoved myself into this project, making each piece perfect, specifically designed for her. When it was over, that pause in time where I wasn't constantly busy with things that needed to be handled imminently, that pause in time would have killed me if it weren't for the men I'd like to kill right now.

It's difficult to keep a calm expression while accepting the tumbler of whiskey from Samantha with a tight smile.

I wouldn't have seen them if I'd stayed in the pool room. I try to remember how long they've been out here, but my mind is fucked.

My pace drags slowly as I stop at the end of the bar, staring down my best friends. I've thought of seeing Sophie again so many fucking times. Never once did I imagine Brett and Ryan would be chatting with her in my own damn bar when the moment came.

Ryan's too close to her. After he slips off his jacket, he places his hand on her shoulder and they both laugh. My eyes narrow as I watch, and my fists clench involuntarily.

My gaze lingers on the curve of her neck and the way she shivers when he takes his hand away from her bare skin. She's mine. At one time, she was nothing but mine.

There's a hint of a blush on her cheeks as they lean against the bar. He always liked her; all of my friends did. At least Brett isn't hovering over her. I could still punch the grin off his face right now, though.

Checking my phone, I make sure they didn't send a message that she was here. They didn't. She's right here, and they didn't tell me.

An agonizing mix of emotions stirs inside of me. Questions ricochet in my head and they don't stop.

When did she get here? Why is she at the bar with them? Were either of them going to tell me? The jealousy that creeps up on me, making my hands tingle when they form white-knuckled fists as Ryan clinks his glass with Sophie's, is unreasonable. He'd never go for her.

I know Ryan, and I know Sophie. He'd never do that shit to me and neither would Sophie. But maybe he knew she'd be here? If any of us would have known, it would be Brett. His sister tells him everything, but he would have told me. The anger rises as I question why no one told me. *How fucking long has she been in New York?*

It doesn't matter; none of the questions barreling through my mind matter either. I'm already striding toward them, hearing her sweet laugh ring in my ears before I can even think straight.

I've built this bar from scratch and been in here a million times, but it's never felt so small, so tight, so damn suffocating.

A new song with a slow beat starts up, and it makes the sound of my shoes thudding on the floor seem that much louder. That much more foreboding.

Brett spots me first of the three of them. The second his eyes reach mine, he grabs his drink and leaves, nodding at me with a knowing grin.

My pulse quickens, but I control it all, forcing myself to calm down as I move to her left, since Ryan's on her right. She looks so damn small between the two of us. She's always been a short little thing.

With a soft smile still flirting on her lips, she peeks over her shoulder to see who's invading her space just as I'm dragging the stool back, getting it the hell away from me. Everything needs to get the fuck back.

She's here. The whole goddamn world needs to pause until I know why, how long she's staying, and how I can keep her this time. I'm not letting her go.

Her gaze catches mine and her breathing noticeably hitches. I see it. I see her chest rise, and I can hear her swallow.

Her lips part, and the glass in her hand nearly falls as she tries to set it back on the bar. Her eyes and both of her hands move to the drink and as her attention shifts to it, I give Ryan a nod. A nod that says, get the fuck away, I've got her now.

His asymmetric smile and the way he slaps the bar and barely gives Sophie a goodbye before taking off behind us tells me everything I need to know.

"Glad you're back, Soph," Ryan says evenly and keeps my gaze, letting his smile grow as he heads back to the pool room to join Brett and Cody.

He always said she would come back, that eventually she'd return. He kept me from chasing her all the way across the country. They all did. Any other time, they would have told me to go to her.

The last time was different, though. I didn't know what happened. I had no fucking clue until it was too late. They told me to give her time, and I did.

The pang in my chest doesn't go unnoticed, but I can't focus on it. All I can do is watch Sophie, observe her and figure out what her next move is.

I'm not letting her run this time. So she'd better think of something else.

Sophie spins all the way around on her seat, her eyes going wide as she watches Ryan's back and realizes she's all alone with me. Her throat tightens as she swallows and the color drains from her face.

Good.

She licks her bottom lip, keeping her gaze down before she peeks back up at me.

Her lips part, but no words come.

It takes a beat, a tick of a clock, a crackle of the fire before she relaxes even the slightest.

A nervous laugh escapes from her lips and she slowly takes her seat again, slipping her slender fingers around the thin stem of her glass.

Instantly the air turns easier, hotter.

For a moment, a short moment while Ryan was here, it felt easy. It felt like I had her back already. But in this second, it all slips away.

Shifting my weight to my left and then right, getting comfortable where I am and giving her a moment, I lean forward on the bar. My chin rests on my knuckles, my thumb brushing against my bottom lip as I stare her down. Her blue eyes are deep enough to get lost in, but she's the one who looks like she's drowning. It only lasts for a moment until her confidence comes back. But I saw it. I know I did.

"You're back?" I question her.

The roaring fire behind her highlights every inch of her expression when she nods, not saying a word, not even looking at me and instead lifting the pink drink to her lips.

I can hear the glass hit the bar top and every other fucking noise in this place until she brings those doe eyes to mine and says, "Yeah, I'm back."

I have to control every inch of my expression so I don't reveal a damn thing. She can't tell that I'm getting hotter by the second, and my cock is getting harder.

"For how long?" I ask, and my voice is even and calm, not giving anything away. My nerves prick up my spine, every impulse I have pushing me to slam my lips against hers.

I remember something Ryan told me once.

She doesn't leave you when she knows she's yours.

It took me a long fucking time to really get what he meant. When I finally realized how true those words were, it was too late.

Her eyes drop to her cocktail before they meet my gaze again and she answers, "I got a job here… I think I'm staying."

Before I can say anything, she cuts me off. "Can I ask you something?"

Giving her a nod, I stare into her beautiful eyes, riddled

with pain I need to erase.

"Are you angry at me? Brett and Ryan..." she breathes out deeply, looking away and pushing the hair out of her face before adding, "they said you wouldn't be angry or upset if you saw me, but I... I know we didn't leave things off... in a friendly way."

"I'm feeling a lot right now, but neither of those things. I missed you, Soph."

I hold her gaze for as long as I can, making sure she feels it. This well of emotion I feel inside of me. "I'm not angry," I add and stop myself from telling her that I'm hurting. I've been hurting since the day she left.

"You need a place to crash?" I ask her, changing the subject as quickly as I can, and she lets out a small laugh at my question.

Pushing her hair back, she lets a sweet smile play at her lips and says, "Sorry, Ryan bought us shots and I think mine's hitting me now."

The air shifts between us. It's easier, less tense, and I fucking love it.

"I don't need a place to crash... I finally got one of those, you know?" Her voice is even, but there's a hint of the playfulness she used to give me back then. In the very beginning of it all. Back to a place I wish we could go.

"I heard you were staying with Brett's sister, but I didn't know about New York?" I don't know how my voice is so level. How everything is so calm on the surface.

She hesitates, as if she doesn't want to tell me. *I know she isn't with someone else.* I'll fucking kill Brett if she is. He told me he'd let me know. Trish tells him every single thing. My expression must've slipped because when Sophie looks up at me she shakes her head slightly, answering my unspoken question.

She's quick to place her small hand over mine, comforting me. She always did that. Even if she didn't do it on purpose, it's just a piece of who she is. Having just that little touch makes me miss her even more. Even though she's right here. I still need her to be mine again.

Electricity flows through me and it takes everything in me not to flip my hand over and keep her skin next to mine when she takes her hand away, telling me she got a dream job and they're paying for her place.

"SoHo too," she adds, and then shrugs. "It's a little fancy, but I just have to add my touches to it." I can hear the pride in her voice.

She's staying in SoHo. Some of the tension leaves my body. She's in a safe area, and she's back for good.

"Like this place. It's all fancy and chic in this area, but I like it."

"You like the bar?" I ask her as I roll up the sleeves of my button-down shirt. My forearms flex as I tuck the cuff links into my pocket and then order us a round. Whiskey for me, and another of what she's drinking for her.

Sophie nods sheepishly, her confidence slipping as the

drinks land in front of us.

"You look good in this bar," I tell her, holding her gaze and watching how she can't help but to smile. When her teeth sink into her bottom lip, I know I've gotten to her, at least a little.

"So do you, in your suit and all. A little better than my hoodie, don't you think?"

"You can wear whatever you want... or nothing at all."

She laughs as I sip my whiskey. "I think the owners might have a problem with that."

My cock is stiff as I imagine her lying on this bar right now. Naked and bared to me in the late night with the doors locked. New York never sleeps, but I'd kick everyone out and let them fade away on the streets as I fucked her right here, watching her hair spread across the bar as she screamed out my name with every thrust.

"I wouldn't mind it," I tell her, not hiding the desire in my voice. She'd do it too. The old her would do it, strip down right here. As long as I turned the lights off. We'd still be able to see the lit streets behind us, but they wouldn't be able to see all the way back here. I'd fuck her hard enough for them to hear her though.

"You're bad," she tells me, but that flirtatious smile is still there. That tension between us rises higher and higher as we slip back into old habits.

"So are you."

Her mouth drops open in disbelief, and she has no fucking

clue what it does to me. "I am not," she says defensively, but she doesn't realize she's scooting closer.

"You like it, that makes you worse." Her smile widens to a full-blown grin, but she merely licks her lower lip and doesn't respond.

I tease her even more and say, "Maybe just bad for me? Is that it?"

Her fingers toy with the rim of her glass. "You are so bad."

"Tell me you love it." I give her the command, but I'd beg her to admit it to me. So I'll know I'm not the only one of us that's crazy for what we had. What we can have tonight.

"I won't lie," she says and shrugs. "I love it."

"Say it."

"I love how dirty you are." The blush that creeps into her cheeks makes her look so innocent.

"Only for you." The words leave me, and her sexy grin slips as my heart pounds and I turn to the alcohol.

"To your new job and your new place," I say as I lift up my shot glass and wait for her to respond.

"You just want to get me drunk so you can fuck me."

"I'll be fucking you either way, Soph." The comment comes from me without hesitation. I bite my tongue to keep from telling her that I'll be punishing her too. She's fucking mine.

"Is that what you think?" she asks me teasingly, although there's a hint of worry woven in. "You buy me a drink and you get to fuck me again?"

Tension crackles between us. She's thinking too much. *Just let it be, Sophie. Let it be.*

"I think you wouldn't be flirting with me like this if you didn't miss me." I hesitate to tell her everything else, but I let some of it slip as I add, "I think you know how much I've missed you. I think you missed me too."

"Maybe," she answers quietly, her fingers still playing with the stem of her glass.

"Let's get out of here then. Or maybe I can clear out the bar, and we can be alone for a minute."

She huffs in disbelief, "Of course you would think to clear out the bar." With a roll of her eyes, she takes another sip of her drink.

"It's my bar, so I can do what I want with it." Instead of looking impressed, she glances at me and then drops her gaze to the glass in her hand.

"Congratulations," she says, but she's quiet and then she visibly swallows.

The lack of excitement is obvious. "I forgot how ..." she trails off and lets out a long breath rather than finishing her thought, then simply shakes her head. "I'm sorry, Madox. I'm really happy for you. You're doing great and this place is really beautiful."

"Why do you look like I just insulted you?"

"Does Trisha know you own this place?" she asks me and that's when it hits me that she was going to avoid me.

"Brett knows," I answer her and she nods slightly and

then looks past me at the pool room.

"I've got to go," she tells me in a single breath; I can practically hear her heart racing now. My hand catches her hip as she slips off the barstool, trying to get around me.

"No, you don't. Don't run from me."

"Don't tell me what to do," she snaps back loud enough for two people to focus their attention on us. My grip slowly lifts from her to my tumbler, although my gaze doesn't wander from hers. I've never known how far to push with her. It's always too much or too little and she's full of fireworks, ready to go off with the slightest provocation.

"I'm sorry," she whispers. "I haven't slept and I wasn't expecting this. I'm--"

"Caught off guard?" I question her. When she nods I tell her, "I wasn't expecting it either. I wasn't expecting you to leave in the middle of the night three years ago, either."

"I'm not doing this right now, Madox. I'm not fighting or dealing with... all that right now."

"The last thing I want to do is fight," I tell her carefully, watching how she absorbs every word. "I didn't mean to put you on edge."

"You always put me on edge, Madox. You are everything and I am so small in comparison. You own New York and I've never had my own place, or even a car. I've been scared to see you for years and you just strode over and told me you want to fuck me. No... no, you said you *will* be fucking me." She corrects herself.

"I'm not taking back that last statement." I speak calmly, letting her know what I want. None of her concerns matter. They've never mattered to me.

"Of course you're not."

"Did you miss me?" I question her with the only thing that is of concern.

"Yes."

"Do you want me now?" I ask her and she nods, her chest rising higher with a deeper breath. "Then tell me the truth. Why are you trying to leave me again?" I ask her, steadying her as she stares up at me with wide eyes.

She breathes out her answer like it's the only truth she's ever known. "You make me feel like I should run."

"Don't run tonight."

Sophie's already shaking her head, her eyes closed tight as she gets ready to bite back with another argument, another reason we shouldn't get together tonight. Another reason she shouldn't be mine. I can already see it.

That's not the girl I want tonight. We can fight tomorrow. Tonight I only want her screaming in pleasure. I miss her too much. I *need* her too much.

She was never good at fighting after I fucked her. She just needs to remember that.

My hands tangle in her hair as I crash my lips against hers. The electricity, the sparks that flew with just her hand on mine earlier intensify.

At first she's stiff, her small hands nearly pushing against my chest, but then she moans, parting her lips and running her fingertips up to my neck, pulling me closer to her as I slip my tongue between the seam of her soft lips.

Her mouth is warm and inviting as she presses her body against mine, and I have to groan. It comes from deep inside of me. I haven't felt like this in years. This primal need to get lost in bed with her.

Her nails scratch down my neck softly, making me that much harder for her. With her breasts pressed against my chest, she lolls her head back to breathe.

My eyes open slowly, focused on her swollen lips and her half-lidded eyes.

"Let me tell you what I want," I say, barely keeping my voice even. I can feel eyes on us and I know some of them belong to my employees, but they can mind their own fucking business.

My statement brings Sophie back to the present from wherever she's wandered. She blinks away the desire from her eyes and nods slightly. The intensity still crackles between us as I tell her, "I want you to come home with me."

"That's a bad idea," she answers in merely a whisper. Her eyes reach mine and she tells me, "*You're* a bad idea."

"You've called me worse," I answer her and lean down just slightly, enough so I can brush my lips against hers.

She's the one who kisses me this time as I pull away,

getting up on her tiptoes to steal a quick but deep kiss. Both of my arms wrap around her and I lower my forehead to hers, not breaking her gaze.

She has the upper hand here, but I know it will change soon. It can't change soon enough.

"We can go back to your place." The words are sinful on her lips.

"Good. We're going to get one thing out of the way in the cab ride. Finish your drink; you're going to need it."

Chapter 4

Sophie
Seven Years Ago

"I've never been with anyone," I tell Madox afterward. My insecurities destroy all the little bits of happiness I just felt last night.

"I like that," is all Madox responds before brushing the hair from my cheek and then kissing me again. He does it in a way where I feel his touch everywhere. From his lips pressed against mine, to his warmth flowing down my skin. And then even lower.

He doesn't say anything else, but he keeps kissing me. Maybe I should ask more questions, but I'm afraid of the answers.

I don't know what I am to him. I know I don't want this to change. It can't last, but I don't want it to change.

Today

I wasn't going to down the drink Madox ordered, but fuck it. One more isn't going to push me over the edge. Besides, I'm with Madox and whenever I'm with him, there is no edge. All I do is free fall when I'm with him.

All my best-laid plans of avoiding him are shot to hell.

I have to remind myself that it's still a fresh start for me, and I'm still focusing on my career, even if I lose my mind and do stupid things whenever I get within five feet of this man.

By the time Madox opens the cab door for me and the night air is blowing against my face, the alcohol is humming in my blood, just like my desire for him to use me.

Maybe it's odd, but I feel like I deserve to be used by him, like it's been a long time coming.

I'm still going to claim I have boundaries and self-respect. There's nothing wrong with wanting to be fucked though, right?

With my hand in Madox's, I lower myself to the seat and pretend like his thumb brushing along my wrist isn't everything I've missed.

Simple touches, the sweetness of it.

My heart longs for something more, but I tell it to shut up. I don't want to think. I think too much when it comes to him. Or maybe I don't think enough. Maybe I overthink nothing with him.

One thing I know for certain is when he's close to me, all I can think about is pleasing him. I have an innate need to please him. I want to know more than anything that he's happy with me – even though I'm well aware it's not a healthy thought to have.

I'm left alone in the backseat to settle my wristlet in my lap as he rounds the car, preparing to take me back to his place, and that small truth forms a lump in my throat. For a second, I nearly jump out of the cab and into the street. He makes me feel like everything, yet at the same time, so obviously inferior. Nothing will ever change that, the power imbalance is simply too drastic. It always has been.

His door is open before I can move, and he gives the cab driver his address.

"Lie down, it'll help with your headache," Madox tells me and I'm slow to register what he's said. The realization surprises me and then excites me. This isn't the first time we've fooled around in a cab. "If you're still feeling hot, take off your hoodie." He adds to the cab driver, "She had a little too much to drink tonight."

I barely get a glance of the driver's gaze in the rearview mirror before telling Madox, "I'll just rest my eyes for the ride."

Heat blooms in the pit of my stomach. My fingers tingle as I slowly take off my hoodie, feeling foolish for wearing it and realizing I'm still in the same clothes I wore on the long-ass plane ride over here. All while Madox is dressed in an undoubtedly expensive and custom tailored suit.

Fuck, he is so out of my league it's not even funny. That's been the problem since the beginning; I should be over it by now.

His large hand covers my hip as I lean closer to him.

My first thought is that he wants head. Biting my bottom lip, I start to lower my head, but Madox grabs the back of my neck, guiding me where he wants me, which isn't my nose to his crotch like I was expecting.

I've always thought it was slutty of me to enjoy giving him a blow job. Even if it turned me on like nothing else to have such a powerful man lose all control when I went down on him. Maybe that's why I'm slightly disappointed.

With my breasts pressed to his thigh and my cheek laying on the leather of the seat, Madox commands me in a low voice to look at the back of the seat and stay quiet.

My heart races as I obey him, waiting with the anticipation only growing hotter and hotter. Draping the hoodie over my midsection and ass, Madox slips his hand under the fabric and deftly undoes the button and zipper to my jeans. The music in the cab is all I can hear, but adrenaline races through me as I wonder if the cab driver can tell what Madox is doing.

With his left hand on my shoulder, and his right under the privacy of the hoodie, I peek up at Madox to see him looking straight ahead and seemingly disinterested.

Even as he shifts my jeans down an inch and then another, slowly exposing my ass to him even though the garment around my waist covers it from any prying eyes.

I've never done anything else with anyone. Nothing.

Madox was my first and only. And I would do *anything* with Madox.

He's fucked me in bathrooms, dressing rooms and back alleys. He's eaten me out at restaurants and I've given him head in towering skyscrapers when he was just taking over his company. So him playing with me in a cab? It does nothing but make me even needier for him than I already am.

I can hear the lace of my underwear tear as Madox asks the cab driver to turn up the music, telling him it's one of his favorites. I doubt he's ever even heard this song before. He's shoving his fingers through the lace and ripping my panties from me when he thanks the driver. With my forearms acting as a pillow for me, I keep my head facing the backseat, but stare up at Madox's strong stubbled jaw.

"Feeling better, sweetheart?" he asks me casually as he shoves a finger inside of my pussy. My lips form a perfect O as a spike of wanton need shocks my system and I hesitate before answering him, "No, I think I need a moment more."

Madox smirks at my response, his dark eyes glinting with want and hunger until he breaks my gaze and acts like he isn't doing anything at all. He watches the driver and then asks him to turn the music up louder so he doesn't fall asleep, all the while playing with me, moving my arousal from my core to my clit. Rubbing and stroking, pushing his fingers in and curling them before dragging them out, slowly lighting me to a smoldering fire.

"We'll be home in twenty and I'll take care of you then." He talks to me as if we're a couple, a loving couple, like I'm merely hungover and he's caring for me. When he strokes his thumb with ruthless pressure over my clit, I bite down on my lip to keep from being any more obvious than this already is.

His fingers inside of me, although they fill me and feel like heaven, are fucking offensive, because I remember all too well what his dick can do to me. I want *him*. He's only teasing me.

He pushes in and out of me before going back to playing with my clit in a mix of gentle and hard caresses, but never letting me get off. He leaves me breathing heavier and waiting for something more.

He's quick to slide his fingers back inside of me and my upper body begs to arch, but his hand in between my shoulder blades keeps me down.

"Don't worry, I won't leave you waiting for long," he whispers when I peek up at him through my lashes. I can hardly hear him and I know for certain the cab driver can't hear a word we're saying. My warm breath lingers in the air between my face and the leather of the back of the seat.

"Madox," I whine. I actually freaking whine with impatience. As the heat rises up my chest to my cheeks with embarrassment, Madox's gaze catches fire. The deep greens brighten and the gold flecks flicker to life. The way he looks at me makes my heart race inside my chest. It always has.

"I fucking love to hear you beg," he mutters beneath his breath and then lowers his head, bringing his lips to my ear. As he talks, his words cause a shiver to run down my spine, and send nothing but heat to my core. "I'm going to take care of you because I want to. But this right now, this is because I need to."

The spark in his eyes steals the air from my lungs. And just then, he curves his fingers, pushing his knuckles against my front wall and I nearly combust on the spot. All rational thought leaves me, my voice leaves me, and my body begs to fall off the cliff of my impending release.

He grinds his knuckles, pressing them against that sinful spot inside of me all while he stares down at me, pushing me closer and closer to the edge.

"You got in a cab three years ago and left me. Every fucking time you sit your pretty ass in a cab, I want you to feel this. Feel how fucking good it is to be mine."

I can't move or do anything but feel the fire build inside of me as he rips the orgasm from me, gripping the back of my neck and pinning my face against the back of the seat as I cum.

It's not until I pull back, sucking in a deep breath of air and looking up at Madox, still impeccably dressed and looking completely unbothered, that he glances back down at me, and pushes his fingers in even deeper.

Minutes pass in silence, and I struggle with the torturous need to moan, but I merely shove my face into the seat and focus on not grinding into his hand.

Madox leans down, just as I'm so close to another release. So close to feeling that warmth spread through my body in a wave that crashes through me, destroying all logic.

"I need to fuck you on a plane as soon as humanly possible. So fucking hard that if you ever think about getting on one without me again, you'll feel me throbbing between your legs."

He drags out every bit of my orgasm, making it last impossibly long, rubbing my hard clit all the while. I'm left shaking in his lap, with my arousal slick between my thighs when the cab slows at the gate to Madox's place, giving me only a minute up his driveway to pull my pants back up over my ass.

"The second we get inside," Madox whispers in my ear, "take your clothes off. They belong on the floor."

Chapter 5

Madox
Seven Years Ago

"You want me to do what?" She blushes when she asks me. Her eyes are wide and her smile grows broader.

"You heard me," I tell her rather than repeat myself. I'm so fucking hard for her. I'll never have enough.

"Madox," she says, and she's trying to sound admonishing, maybe offended, but she can't with that sinful smile as she bites down on her lower lip.

"We can do that, or we can do something else," I offer her, whispering as I brush her hair back so I can see the dip of her collar. "What do you want to do, Soph?" I ask her, willing to do anything and everything.

She says the sexiest thing she could right now and I don't even *think she knows it as she answers, "Whatever you want, I want."*

Today

She's walking too slow; kissing, gripping me, and stumbling every which way.

It's been too long since her ass has hit my bed. Too long since I've tasted her from my fingers. And it's too easy to lift her up, let those sexy legs of hers wrap around my waist and carry her up the stairs to my bedroom.

"I want you on your knees first." My words are accompanied by the hiss of my leather belt being pulled from the loops of my suit pants. The belt buckle clangs as it carelessly hits the floor and I can't be bothered to look at it.

I unbutton my shirt, all the while my gaze is focused on Sophie and how her hips sway slightly as she crawls to the middle of the bed – *my* bed – until she's happy where she is, raising her ass in the air and lowering her cheek to the white comforter.

With my chest rising and falling, my pulse picking up and the need to slam myself into her riding me hard, I memorize the sight of her flushed skin and the way she nuzzles into the bed with a soft moan, teasing me as she waits for what's to come.

It fucking kills me not to take her hard and rough and force her to scream my name the way she should have been for years right now, but I want this to be perfect.

"Hands behind you." I give her the command while I kick off my pants. She reaches her hands back, setting them beside her ankles, and I tsk. "Play with your cunt."

Her blush turns vibrant and travels up her chest and cheeks as she moves her hands slowly, teasing herself and letting goosebumps kiss along her bare skin.

Her hands still haven't reached her pussy by the time I step up to the end of the bed and give her one hard slap on her ass. She gasps and jumps immediately. Her fingers fly to that greedy pussy of hers too, rubbing her swollen nub and running along her slit. It glistens when her back arches and she settles back down from the single slap.

I admire the red mark, tracing it with my fingers and listening to her moan of pleasure from the simple touch that hovers over her heated skin.

"Have you forgotten I like things done quickly?" I ask her, toying with her and leaning down to suck her cunt, even over her fingers, still rapidly moving in circles around her clit.

"No," she says softly. "Just making you wait even longer for what you want," she tells me with a smirk playfully pulling at her lips.

Stroking my cock, I climb on the bed behind her and then lean down, licking her slit and pushing my fingers back inside of her roughly. The tortured gasp and the way her back bows are everything I wanted.

"I'm done waiting." Even though my words hold impatience, I want her to get off again. Every time she cums is a fucking victory for me. The next one drags out longer, it hits her harder, and it comes so much more easily. "I'm not going to stop fucking you tonight until you're able to cum just from a single lick along your clit."

Her eyes close at my words, and as if I've commanded it, she cums on my fingers. That's three in the last hour. I want more.

"Arch your back; I want your ass up higher." She listens and obeys, even though she's still shaking. In bed it's always easy between Soph and me. She knows I'll make it good for her. And I know she'll love me for it.

It's when we aren't physically together that she doesn't trust I'll be good for her. I can change that. I can be better this time. I will be. She'll see it. She'll stay this time. I know she will.

With a hand splayed on Sophie's hip, my fingers dig into her flesh as I slam myself inside of her heat.

Fuck, she feels so tight. I struggle to hold back my murmur of pleasure from feeling her heat wrap around my cock.

Pushing myself deeper inside of her, I let out a rough groan from my chest. My lips graze the crook of her neck and then the shell of her ear.

"Fuck, I missed you," I whisper and it's her undoing.

She's already cumming again. Spasming around my cock as her body shivers beneath me.

Even consumed by pleasure, a smirk forms on my lips. I

leave an open-mouth kiss along her jaw and then her cheek, waiting for her orgasm to rock through her body. She's breathing heavily, her lips parted and body still trembling when I pull out just slightly and then push in even deeper, fully seated inside of her.

"I was going to fuck you slowly, to tease you and torture you for making me wait this long to have you again," I whisper my words and slowly her eyes open. Her baby blues find mine, and I hold them in my gaze.

"I've missed you too much not to have you like I selfishly want."

Sophie lifts her head just slightly, not speaking and only giving me a single kiss before falling back to the bed, barely able to brace herself with her forearms.

And then I ravage her. Keeping my promise. The last time I touch her, she cums one last time with a single flick of my tongue to her clit and nothing more.

Chapter 6

Sophie
Seven Years Ago

There's this ominous feeling I get every time I leave or he leaves. A feeling like this is how it'll be forever, like this is what I'm supposed to have. A world without him.

I can't explain the anxiousness and the insecurity. I can explain why I feel so unworthy though. Anyone could look between the two of us and write an essay on that matter.

I think that's why he doesn't call me his girlfriend – I'm not. I'm not his girlfriend.

"Hey." Madox's voice surprises me, as does his grip on my chin forcing me to look up at him. "You okay?"

"Yeah," I reply, but I can barely breathe as I answer him. Swallowing thickly, I try to come up with a reason to give him *that can hide the truth, but I'm struggling. I'm struggling with everything.*

With his arms wrapped around me, it all goes away. He has that power – to touch me and let everything else melt to nothing. Everything else is nothing compared to him.

It's when he leaves that I realize what the feeling is. It's the feeling you get when you know it's only a matter of time before it all ends. When it does, I'll be left with nothing.

Today

Sometimes when people meet, they'll never be the same again. There's a piece of the other person that stays with you forever.

I remember this bed, the way it feels, the way it smells like Madox. I remember his house and how it was freezing cold and empty in a way that always made me sad for him. I remember this room, his bedroom, how it was the only place that felt like him, with its dark, textured wallpaper and thick curtains that keep out all the light and sound.

Last night at the bar, Madox gave me more than he gave me all the years we were together. He was quiet and reserved back then, and he never would have told me how he felt. I never knew how he felt. Definitely not that he missed me.

I always knew I loved him, but even so, I also knew he'd let me leave and never come for me. That's not what someone does when they miss you, let alone when they love you.

For years we were off and on, so there were plenty of times to miss each other. I always went back to him. He was the only man I was ever with because deep down, I thought he cared for me at least, even if it wasn't the same kind of love that I had for him.

That's why I sent him a message the morning before I left for good three years ago. After he fucked me in the alley. After I fled back to my apartment, after we fought, after I cried myself to sleep, knowing it was over for good. Even still, before I left with Trish, I gave him one last chance. I texted him before packing what little I had in my apartment for the flight, and I asked him to tell me if he wanted me to stay. I told him I was going to San Francisco, but if he wanted me to stay, I would. I just needed him to tell me how he felt. I needed to know if it was one sided and hear him say it.

He didn't text me back at all. That's who Madox is. Or at least it's who he was.

He never gave me any verbal indication of any sort that he wanted me. All I needed was for him to tell me he wanted me to stay, and he never did.

Not until last night.

Maybe I'm a fool to fall back into bed with him. But hearing those words, "I want you"... it did something to me.

Like finally having your wish come true.

It took me back to the first night I met him and through all the years we spent together when those words would have changed everything. And to the first night, when I knew he wanted me to stay and I knew he cared for me. He didn't even know me, but I knew he cared. He had to have cared, in order to do what he'd done.

That night was both hell and a living nightmare. But for me, it was the start to what I thought could be a fairytale.

I remember that entire month and the days after so vividly. I was only seventeen, soon to be eighteen, and I'd never heard the name Madox Reed before. It all happened because I had to pee, if you can believe that. Well, maybe not. Maybe it all happened because my stepdad was a dick. I wouldn't stand for it, not even when my mother would.

I guess that was really the straw that broke the camel's back. I'd reached my limit, and there was no going back. He yelled "cunt" when he punched the window as my mother drove away, weeks before the night from hell.

My mom had left him before so many times. It was like a yearly holiday. They fought a lot, damn near constantly. And every once in a while my mother would have enough and leave, taking me with her.

She'd always go back to him though, and after this particular fight she did just that. We'd spent the longest time at her friend's house. Two weeks exactly, which was the most time she'd ever stayed away, but just like always, she'd gone back. She forgave him.

I didn't.

I couldn't get the fear out of me from that single moment. It lingered every time I got into my mother's car.

When she was leaving him and driving away, I was sitting in the passenger seat, looking straight ahead and trying not to show anything at all. No tears, no anxiety. My mother was a wreck and she needed me to move quickly, to pack my bag and get in the seat – just like we had before. Through the yelling, through the fighting, I kept it all bottled deep inside, where it shook and shook and shook. Like a can of Coca-Cola waiting to explode. My heart raced when I saw him come out of the house as the engine thrummed and my mother rubbed haphazardly under her eyes. Her mascara smeared, but she didn't care. It wasn't like she could see it at all. Her face was red and there was barely any makeup left from all the wiping she did.

She put the car into drive as he screamed something at her. All the windows were closed, but my mother screamed back regardless. Still fighting, even though she was leaving.

They did that to each other. They fought and pushed each other away. It even got physical sometimes. As we took off and I stared straight ahead, trying to ignore the pain in both their voices, my stepdad punched the window – my window – and yelled "cunt" as my mother drove away.

Even in the memory, my body jolts.

The window was closed. Every time I remember it, I think about how hard he hit it. I can't tell for sure anymore if it was as hard as it felt back then.

I never cried when we left him. My mother needed me to be strong. But back then if I allowed myself to dwell on that thud of the window, the sight of his fist, even the word that romance novels have taught me to love so much because it's used so differently... that four letter C-word, I cried and I kept crying. I couldn't stop.

Madox used that word too, weeks later. He didn't know what had happened – he didn't know I hated the word, he didn't know the word made my body shake in a way I wish I could control – and he said it in bed. But when he said it, it was with a reverence that singed the memory of what it used to mean into nothing but ash.

The way he used it was sinful and decadent. It's the only way the word should ever be used.

Because of him and my books, I love the word now; I'm over the power that word had held over me, but back then it brought me so much fear. Just the memory of how it was used was enough to make up my mind.

That wouldn't be for weeks though. I had no idea who Madox was at the time.

When she went back to my stepdad, I didn't.

Legally, I was almost an adult, and I had a car of my own, although it'd been at the shop at the time of their latest breakup. I told them I wasn't going to live like that. I watched my mother break down in a way I've never seen, and I watched my stepfather's eyes gloss over, although he eventually screamed at me when I didn't accept his half-assed apology. Just like he screamed at my mother.

All I had was a car, a part-time job on the weekends, and about $50 in cash. I figured I'd sleep in the car. It was spring, so it was warm enough. I could park a couple of blocks from my work at a vacant house for sale. No one would mind.

I would make it work. Because there was no way I was going back to that house to listen to them scream at each other.

Fifty dollars would last me until payday if I only bought stuff from the dollar menu at fast food places. I wouldn't need gas, because I'd walk everywhere. I was so sure of myself and if I lived in a perfect world, I could have made it work.

But life is no vacuum-sealed safe room. There are other people existing, watching... waiting.

The third night, I was so damn lonely. My mother called, but her voice was drowned out by the stern voice in the background telling her to put her foot down and not to contradict him. If I was going to make her choose between her husband and her daughter, then I was the problem. Maybe I was.

After all of this happened, I never chose between them again. I came and went and simply saw my mom and stepdad for who they were. A couple who fought, and I wouldn't stand in the middle any longer. It was easier to love them, and easier for them to love me that way. We were never the same though.

The eighth night was my breaking point.

The guys at the corner store knew I was coming in just to use the bathroom because the school was closed at night. They told me I couldn't come in anymore unless I was going to buy something. I was down to less than ten dollars; it turned out three dollars a meal wasn't enough. It was late and dark, I was hungry, and I needed to go to the bathroom. Everywhere else was closed, which is why I drove there.

A few streets down from where I parked was mostly vacant. It led to a few houses and a bar. I walked behind a house for sale, intending on just doing my business. I needed to pee or my bladder would burst; I was on the verge of maybe crying because I felt so stupid and so alone. It would have been just that, and then I'd go back to my car and curl up under the blanket and cry myself to sleep again, wondering how my mother could choose him when I chose her every time. It would have been, but I wasn't alone.

I knew something was wrong the second I squatted down in the darkest area behind the shed to pee as quick as I could. It was quiet, way too quiet until I heard their voices.

There were four guys, each holding partially empty bottles. One had covered his in a paper bag, but the others didn't care if everyone could tell they were drinking cheap beer.

The pee dribbled down my leg as I pulled my pants up, stopping midstream. My heart hammered and I swear it tried to leave me, tried to climb up my throat and run. I was too afraid to be embarrassed or ashamed like I'd been when I crept back here hoping no one would see. It never occurred to me how bad things can get and how quickly a situation can turn.

They knew I was there; that was obvious because they didn't break their stride as they pushed open the gate of the fence leading to the backyard of the house for sale. Words escaped me, breath abandoned me.

I just stood there full of dread, with the shed to my left and a privacy fence behind me.

Four of them, and one of me. Their smiles were telling, even in the darkness. The wolf whistles, the coarse laughs. I thought I knew fear before that night. I thought wrong.

"Yo!" I remember the word being shouted from my right, way down the road and I turned to look, breaking my gaze from the four intruders. Still not having moved, not having spoken, the true terror having turned every piece of me into a numb statue. Another group of people down the street fucking around and laughing were either coming or going, probably from the bar. But I could hear them too.

"Help!" How the word came from me, I have no idea. The first time I screamed it, the expressions on the faces of the men who'd followed me changed, these four young, drunk men who had waited for me to get out of my car so they could follow me and trap me. The second time I screamed out toward the stray voice I heard in the distance, I took half a step forward, feeling the adrenaline in my blood urging me to fight back. I knew someone was there; I just didn't know if they would come and help me. I knew I couldn't help myself though. I knew whatever happened if they didn't save me, was going to be horrific. So I screamed louder and louder, begging for help until my voice was raw.

The closest man grabbed me, trying to cover my mouth and I fought the best I could. I remember the way his grimy hand felt over my face. I bit him, scratched him, kicked out and hit his shin. The next time I screamed for help, the word was ragged and hot tears were streaming down my cheeks. He was so much bigger than me.

I was tired and weak, and I was so fucking scared.

I didn't have to keep fighting though. There were only three guys down the street who had heard me, but they came.

My knights in shining armor were older than me, but younger than the guys who'd tried to hurt me. They were all wearing the same jacket and one of them threw his off as he saw what was happening and ran. His muscles bulged under the streetlight and the asshole who still had his hands on me, released me to take off. He hopped over the side fence and I thought my rescuer would do the same the way he was running, but he stopped short as my shoulders jerked forward and I dry-heaved.

I got sick right there. Maybe from the shock or the horror. Maybe because I hadn't eaten. Still, I didn't feel embarrassed or ashamed, because fear clung to me, just like the feeling of that man's hands on me.

Eight nights alone and living with anger and sorrow had been hell, but that night was disgust and fear in a way I'd never felt before. With the shock came the need to throw up. I didn't have anything in me though.

I still remember the way my hero stared at me when I finally lifted my head to look at who had rescued me, the way he pulled back my hair and told me it was all right. He was beautiful, and I was haggard and covered in filth.

"What's your name?" he asked me.

There was a comfort to his tone, his touch. I knew I was disgusting in every sense of the word. I was shaken up, horrified and questioning everything. I hadn't bathed in three days since the last time I was able to use the showers in the locker room at school, I'd peed on myself and my clothes were dirty. Fuck, it was the lowest point in my entire life. Rock bottom had a new meaning for me that night.

He didn't seem to notice or care about any of that, and when he talked to me and put his hand on my arm to comfort me, I didn't either.

"Sophie," I breathed my name and told him, "Sophie Miller."

He offered me the kindest smile, and all the while he rubbed soothing circles along my back. I kept shaking; I couldn't stop, even if inside I felt so warm with him holding me the way he was. "I'm Madox and these are my friends, Cody and Ryan." My gaze shifted to the other guys, both of them watching me and instinctively, I moved closer to Madox.

Madox. The name itself sounded powerful and protective. I whispered it and then looked back up at him. It was a sin to look at him the way I was in that moment. I knew I shouldn't, that I was going to hurt later but just before I could tear my gaze away, he smiled at me. One of those sweet smiles that's genuine and steals all your worries from you.

"Sophie's a beautiful name." The way he said it, I felt beautiful. I felt like someone else. I felt like the night hadn't happened the way it did. The moment was over quickly, with the sound of the other guys quieting down and the sight of them keeping their distance.

I didn't question him at all when he told me, "Come on." I was grateful when he wrapped the jacket he'd thrown down before around my shoulders.

The scent comes back to me at the thought; he smelled clean but woodsy as he held me close to his side. His hands were strong and warm, and he was taller and far more dominating than the other men, but there wasn't an ounce of fear in me.

The other two guys talked to him, their words bouncing around in my head but not being heard as I tried everything in my power to just stop shaking.

I only knew I wasn't okay and something bad must have happened, because I couldn't stop shaking.

I was in so much shock that I didn't even realize I was in the car with them until the doors were closed and we were moving. That's when I freaked out, but Madox shushed me.

He asked me to trust him, and there were no questions after that, only demands. To come inside. To shower and change into his clothes. To this day, I swear someone else took over that night. No sane girl would have blindly listened to strangers like I did, especially when I remember how scared I was of Ryan and Cody. They didn't look at me like Madox did. They didn't know what to make of me, and I didn't know what to make of them.

I came back to it hours later, remembering how Madox had said something at the bedroom door before closing it, leaving me to sleep, and before I passed out.

When I went to sneak out, that's when I realized he'd locked the door from the inside and closed it. I remember how it felt so wrong to unlock it and dare to step out into the hallway. I registered how expensive everything looked only in that moment. I hadn't noticed any of it before.

It was quiet, and the house felt lonely. I found out later that it was empty. Madox had locked my bedroom door and the doors to the house, and they'd all left together. They knew the men who'd tried to hurt me, and they hurt them back.

It's why they didn't run after the guys while I was there.

They didn't need to. They knew where they'd be.

It wasn't worth it though. Madox didn't just hurt the man, he beat him unconscious at a bar and was arrested.

The fucked up thing was that after I went home that early morning, in clothes that weren't mine and didn't fit, without my car and still scared, I told my mother I was sorry – they found out what had happened and I confessed even more of the sordid truth – I told them everything, and it was my stepfather who bailed Madox out of jail.

I felt like I owed him – I owed both of them – more than I could ever repay.

I was a girl who was no one. A girl who knew nothing. A girl who wanted to stand up for something, but fell to the lowest low when on her own. I caused nothing but problems, and I hated myself for it. If I could take it all back, I would've. I wouldn't have shut my mouth and dealt with the pain from hearing my stepfather yell cunt as he punched the window the same way I'd always dealt with them yelling... bottling it up, deep down inside. If I could go back, I'd do that still. Because all the events landed Madox in jail and I went right back to where I was told to go from the beginning.

I tried to forget what happened, but I couldn't. I needed to see them. I needed to thank them and tell them I was sorry too. That's all I was at that point in my life. Sorry.

I saw Madox again a week later, complete with his group of friends, when I finally had the balls to apologize but also thank them. I went back to the large house he'd taken me to, which was practically a mansion, and I waited on the porch for him.

That day changed everything. I wouldn't be the person I am without them.

I can't even imagine what would've happened if they hadn't been walking down the street at that moment. Just the thought of that shed gave me the worst nightmares for months, nightmares where Madox and his friends weren't there.

The nightmares went away though the day after I told Madox about them. It took me months to tell him about them, but when I did, he told me he'd change that. He fucked me against that same shed and told me that was the only memory of the shed that mattered. I stared at the fence where the men had come through and Madox whispered in my ear all the sweet nothings a girl dreams of. Their steps disappeared from my memory and all I could hear was Madox. The hand I felt vanished in place of the pleasure Madox gave me. He kissed every inch of me, made me stare at anything that reminded me of the bad, and in its place, gave me a good I didn't know existed.

It wasn't my first time with him, but it was one of our firsts. It was the first time he took me somewhere other than his bed, and the first time he showed me what depths he would go to in order to erase any pain I had.

He was right too. Nothing else mattered. That was the first time I wanted to tell him I loved him. But I kept quiet. I saved my words like he did, and pretended I was okay with that.

It was wrong that we were together. I knew that. He was older and I wasn't old enough. He was wealthy and had already established himself in a career he was born to dominate. I was nothing and he was everything. I didn't understand why he would want me, but a small part of me hoped it wouldn't change. That was my first problem – not wanting things to change when they were so unbalanced, I would never be able to keep up.

Lying in Madox's arms while staring up at the ceiling fan, every bit of that anxiousness, that regret... that small bit of hope, comes to the surface all over again.

"Should I pretend to be asleep so you can sneak out? Or will you let me buy you coffee?" Madox's voice is calm and even, although his sleepiness is evident in his tone.

Has it really been seven years since all that? Has life really changed so much since then?

"As if you could sleep through me wrestling my jeans over my ass," I mock him as I shift under the comforter, listening to it rustle and pretending like memory lane didn't just tear me down to the girl I used to be. Laying a cheek against his chest, I peek up at him as he chuckles.

It's been so long since I've kissed him, but in my head I always imagined it was everything. The heat, the forcefulness mixed with a tenderness that smoldered with desire. I thought a few months ago that I made him seem larger than life in my memory. That it was all in my head.

But it's real. Every bit of it is real. The way he kisses, the way he does everything, is even better than I remember.

My fingers play with a small smatter of hair on his chest as I wonder if he wants me to stay a little longer, or if I should go. More importantly, I wonder if anything at all has changed.

Chapter 7

Madox
Seven Years Ago

"You don't have to look at me like that," I tell her as she stands there, nervously fidgeting with her fingers.

"I'm sorry--"

"Stop saying you're sorry," I command her without thinking about it. She shouldn't be sorry. I hate that she looks at me like that.

"Okay," she whispers, her wide, deep blue eyes seeking approval from me. I want to take that pain away from her; I want to see her anything other than the way she is now. "I just wanted to tell you, I really appreciate what you did and I'm--" she pauses to swallow and then concludes, "I wish you hadn't gotten in trouble for it."

"I'm fine," I tell her, knowing how much she isn't fine. I almost ask her to come inside. I almost ask her if she wants to, but instead I tell her to come inside and that I'd washed her clothes for her. I deliberately bring her into the game room first, so the guys can see she's here. "You want to let off some steam and play pool or something?" Ryan asks her. I knew he would; he's a shark. Before she can answer, I place my hand on the small of her back and tell her, "I'm only playing if we play in teams."

I hope I never forget the way her expression changes in that moment. Where she realizes no one here wants her to be sorry.

Today

I can still feel her lips kissing down my neck as the waiter pours our coffee. The smell is rich and enticing, but it's nothing compared to my memory of last night. I have to stare at the glass front door of the shop to keep from replaying every second with her in my bed, listening to the chimes of the bells hanging above the door as an older man wearing a newsboy cap enters, pausing to shake out his umbrella.

"The weather sucks today," Sophie says, although her voice is sweet and airy. My eyes drift back to her as she blows across the top of her coffee. Mine's black and hers is only a few shades darker than the cream tablecloth.

As she takes her first sip, I can't take my eyes off of her.

"I want to see you again. Tonight."

My words catch her off guard and she nearly spits her coffee back up. She's frantic as she pulls the napkin from her lap to wipe her mouth.

I don't say a damn thing, only wait for her response once she's set down the napkin.

"Can't we just talk about the weather and pretend like I'm not wearing the same clothes I had on last night?"

"No," I say, and my answer is flat. I know what I want; I'm not accepting anything less. Her hesitation sends a prick of uncertainty down my spine, but I ignore it. I know she feels what's between us just like I do. I know she does. It's always been between us. After the four years she was mine the three years without her has simply been a waiting game. That's all it was. Waiting. I'm done waiting now.

Sophie's smile fades to nothing and she shifts nervously in her seat before glancing at the door.

"Is that so shocking? That I want to see you again?" I ask her, feeling a wretched twisting in my chest. The frustration is more than a hint.

Her eyes reach mine instantly. "That you would say it?...Yes."

Anger simmers as she keeps her blue eyes on mine, prying and searching for God knows what.

"I found myself when I left." A deep breath leaves her as she sighs and picks up her mug to take a sip. "I like the person I am now, and I don't want to go back to what I was."

"Who you were? What was wrong with who you were? You've always been perfect." She softens at my last sentence, visibly so.

"I didn't have a voice." She stares into her mug as she tells me, "I didn't know what I wanted in life."

"What do you want now?"

"I don't want to make the same mistakes as we did before... I know that much."

"I understand. I made mistakes in the past; I know that now. I don't want to fight with you. I don't want to lose you, either." I offer my hand to her, palm up on the small table, and just like I knew she would, Sophie sets her small hand in mine before tracing the lines on my palm with the tips of her fingers. "It doesn't have to be one or the other. I just want to see you again."

"I don't know," Sophie whispers, looking lost and I hate it. I hate it all. I pull my hand away, feeling the chill in the air against my palm. It pairs perfectly with the hollowness in my chest. "You'll ruin me," she answers with a dullness in her voice, a loss of fight yet complete with conviction.

Ruin her. Yes. That's exactly what I want to do. No other man is right for her but me.

Hearing those words on her lips unleashes a part of me

I don't want to hide from her. It's impulsive, but I grab the leg of her chair and drag both it and her closer to me. She squeals, and with the addictive sound she grins broadly. The heat, the tension, it all skyrockets as she bites down on her lower lip and that beautiful blush I love to see creeps onto her cheeks.

"People will see." She barely gets out the excuse before I tell her, "Let them."

"Madox," she says and her whisper is a hushed admonishment, but her smile stays in place as she peeks up at me and then at my lips before giving me a small chaste kiss.

When she breaks away, I wait for her eyes to reach mine and kiss her deeper, cupping her jaw and kissing her the way she deserves to be kissed.

I kiss her until she's breathless, letting the tip of my nose brush against hers and then kissing her once more, quick and soft, to seal the kiss.

"The way you kiss me..." She doesn't finish her sentence, keeping her eyes closed the entire time.

The need to take her right now creeps up on me as she glances at her phone, and it buzzes in her hand until she clicks the screen.

With a reluctant sigh, she tells me, "I have to go; my boss wants to meet for brunch before work tomorrow."

"I want to see you tonight." I leave no room for negotiation in my tone. "We have a lot to talk about. A lot to catch up on."

Picking up her purse, she brushes her hair behind her ear and settles her phone into place, leaving me waiting.

Just as I'm ready to tell her I've waited long enough, she speaks softly. "I'm scared it's going to be just like how it was before."

She'll never know how much it fucking kills me to hear her say that. Every day since she left, I've coveted what we had.

"I don't want to be some weak girl hanging on the arm of a man who's perfectly fine if she walks away," she says, and her voice cracks. "I don't want to fight, Madox."

"We don't have any reason to fight. I'm just taking you to dinner." I feel my throat tighten as I swallow, and the old man from earlier leaves with a to-go cup of coffee in his hand, making the bells jangle again. He steals her attention from me, but when I get it back, she offers me a kind smile.

"I don't remember you being this ... persistent."

"You don't know everything about me, Sophie. I was never okay when you walked away."

She doesn't know how I kept tabs on her when I found out she'd run away. She doesn't know what I thought of her that very first night she slept in my clothes, in my house, either.

"Meet me tonight." Although I've given her an order rather than a request, I'm not sure that she will. Her movements pause, halting the hoodie midair before she slips it on and then nods.

"I'll meet you." Her expression turns soft as she tells me

quietly, "I was dreading seeing you, you know?" She shakes her head as if in disbelief then adds, "But somehow I knew I wouldn't be able to set foot in this city without running into you."

She offers me a kiss on the cheek before she leaves, bells chiming as I watch her walk away, thinking about that first night I met her, the night I saved her, and how everything shifted the first moment I saw Sophie Miller.

She may have dreaded seeing me last night, but there isn't a damn thing I ever dreaded when it came to her except for her walking away. Since the moment I saw her, it's always been her.

"Is she homeless?" Ryan asked me from the front seat of Cody's Mercedes. He asked the question from between tightly clenched teeth, but she heard him anyway, stiffening beside me in the backseat. She was so beautiful. Her vulnerability though, her trusting me, it called to me like nothing had before.

Cody rolled down the windows, letting in the night air as we drove back to our place by the park. It was a smaller place, one owned by Cody's parents, and we used it as our party pad. Brett had stayed back to play video games, but he was the only one there. She'd be safe there; we could keep her safe. I could keep her safe.

"I left my parents' house... my car, fuck..." the small girl

trailed off and whirled around to look out the back window. "My car is back there, just--"

"It can wait," I said, cutting her off. She'd already freaked out once, but she listened to me. She trusted me. At least enough to calm down.

"I don't want to go home." Her words shook like her shoulders did, and when Cody looked back at her, she scooted closer to me. She did that all night, clinging to me like I was her savior whenever anyone looked at her. No one had ever looked at me like that.

She needed a shower, clean clothes and someone to look after her. At least until she stopped shaking.

"Should we call the cops?" Ryan asked, peeking back at me in the rearview mirror.

I shook my head, feeling the familiar anger rise inside. I didn't need the police involved. I already knew what I was going to do. The anger would have taken over, like it used to ever since what happened with my father, but in that second, her side touched mine. She leaned against me, soft and warm and wanting to be held.

She needed me to.

It should anger me that I crave that moment back. She was anything but okay, and I have no right to want to go back there when she was in so much pain.

But no one has ever needed me like she did then.

It took hours before she agreed to sleep in my room at the house. I told her I wasn't letting her sleep in her car, and I thought she'd fight back, but she was too tired. I could see it in her eyes.

I locked the bedroom door before closing it shut... I locked it because I didn't trust myself to leave her alone that night. I wanted to sleep beside her, to be there if something happened, to watch over her. Something was broken inside of her and I recognized it. I just didn't know what.

I wanted to kiss her more than anything. She was younger than me, she was vulnerable and it was wrong. It was fucked up that I craved her like I did. But worse than that, I felt deep inside that she'd kiss me back. She'd do whatever I asked that night, and I didn't trust myself not to ask for more than she could give.

I promised myself in that moment when I locked the door to the guest bedroom, leaving her safe inside, if she ever wanted to walk away, I'd let her. What we had scared me, and I couldn't imagine what it did to her. I thought she'd know I would still be there waiting. How could she not know that?

I didn't take into account that we came from different worlds. She was used to running and fighting. It's what she knew. What I knew was something completely different.

I've never been attracted to anyone like I'm drawn to Sophie. I want to take every bit of her, and that's exactly what I did. Every single piece of her was mine.

She's used to fighting; her mother made sure of that.

When I didn't fight back, she left me.

When I did fight back, she left me.

I know how to hold her when she needs me to, and back then, she needed my touch often. I have no fucking idea how to hold on to her though when she doesn't want it, but I'm not going to back down. I did once, and it left me desolate for three years, waiting for her to come back.

I know she wants me the way I want her. That's the only thing that matters.

Chapter 8

Sophie
Seven Years Ago

I don't want to go home, so I stay here with Madox. I'm not his girlfriend though and that makes me feel a certain way. A way that's uncomfortable. A way that makes me feel ashamed.

I'm afraid to ask him if I can call him my boyfriend. I'm afraid to push him away. His stubble is scratchy when he kisses my bare shoulder and I have to shudder which makes him chuckle behind me.

That sound makes me smile. The sound of him happy.

"Madox?" I whisper, staring ahead at a dresser that isn't mine but one he filled with clothes for me. "What are we?" I don't know what he'll think of the question.

"We don't have to put a label on it, Soph. Just let it be," he *tells me. It's easy for him to let it be. He doesn't understand how I feel. How could he?*

I should tell him, but I'm ashamed, and it's easier to run away from your everything, than it is to know that you've lost it.

Today

Okay, so I got drunk and slept with Madox.

And maybe it was more than sex.

And maybe I'm having a hard time pretending like I don't still have feelings for him even if it's not the same to him. Yes, I know we'll never be able to be together because we simply aren't on equal footing. He's so much more than I will ever be.

So, should I have slept with him last night...? *No.*

If I took a poll, I'm sure half of Manhattan would raise their hand and say they've done the same damn thing or something like it. Well, not with Madox, but with their exes or former lovers. It happens.

I was only tipsy, not drunk, but I'm still going to blame it on Ryan and the shot he bought me. I'm going to kick him in the dick the next time I see him too, for leaving me alone with Madox the second he could. Figuratively, not literally.

He knew what he was doing.

My phone buzzes with yet another message from my nosy

bestie who could have given me a heads-up about last night. She had to have known, although she keeps telling me she had no idea.

So then what? Trisha's text makes me roll my eyes. I only told her I ran into Ryan and Madox last night. She didn't ask about her brother, so something tells me she already knew.

All of her questions this morning have revolved around Madox. That whole crew seems to be seriously invested in knowing the details of what's going on between us. It's like we're their only entertainment and the rest of them are just sitting in a circle, passing around the popcorn.

We hooked up, I text her and then quickly add, *I couldn't help myself.*

"Would you like to order anything while you wait?" The waiter's voice makes me jump in my seat and he apologizes, but I wave it off.

"Just nervous for my first meeting on the job." I shake my head, swallowing thickly before realizing what he asked and reply, "Just water for now, please." As he nods and makes to leave, I'm quick to add, "And a coffee." He smiles and nods.

It's not until he's gone that I look back down at my phone.

I never told you – but he asked about you all the time. I didn't want you to feel guilty.

My fingers hover over the keys, but I don't write anything back. I can't believe she never told me.

I had no idea he ever even thought about me. A little

hurt, along with a lot of betrayal stir inside of me, and I know I shouldn't text her back right now. How could she never tell me?

How could he never tell me either?

Madox is good at telling people what to do, which made us bump heads a lot. It led to some awful moments. It led to some great moments too. He's really good at giving demands; he's shit at talking about how he feels though. At least with me. At least back then.

Emotions swarm in my chest at the thought of him wondering what I was doing and if I would come back. I always walked away because he was so quiet and distant. There are only two times we were together when I felt like he let me in. Like he showed me a piece of him that was just for me. Which was so unfair, because he had all of my pieces. He knew everything about me and every vulnerability.

In all four years we were together, there are only two times he dropped his guard and let me in.

The second and last time was the night he came to my apartment, the night I left him. I sought him out because I knew he could make me feel better and then I ran away, hating myself for using him, hating myself for going back to someone who couldn't give me a commitment. Every low moment I had, I ran to him, and I couldn't keep doing it. Especially not with what had happened that week.

I knew I shouldn't have been with him that night the second he was done fucking me in the alley. By that point I couldn't stand to look at myself in the mirror, so I ran to my ex. The same ex who had never told me he loved me during the four years we were together, the ex who never once called me his girlfriend. The ex I let call me a whore as he fucked me in an alley. It doesn't take a rocket scientist to know I was fucked in the head and needed help.

I knew going to him because I was in pain was wrong. I was falling into an old pattern of behavior, relying on a bad habit simply because I felt a gaping hole in my heart I knew he could fill. And when I realized that, I knew it had to be the last time.

So when he told me he'd enter the bar after me, and back to an old group of friends I'd missed so much since I'd last seen him nearly two weeks prior, I gave him a small smile and kissed the edge of his lips, noting how rough his stubble felt against the pads of my fingertips. He didn't realize it was goodbye, or that I already missed him. I said I'd go to the bathroom first and he should go in before me.

I liked being his whore, his submissive, his... whatever you'd call it. A lot of people called me a lot of things. Both to my face and behind my back. The sex was always amazing, whether it was sweet or dirty; slow and sensual, or hot and rough. But it crossed lines I didn't know how to avoid. And that night, I felt dirty. I felt like I was beneath him in the way I always feared he saw me. I felt like I was only a poor girl he saved once, a pathetic girl who kept coming around because she had no one else. That's how I felt, and although something deep inside my heart screamed it was more than that, there were no words to prove it to me.

I didn't expect anything at all from him when I escaped back to my place, but certainly not him banging on my door, demanding for me to tell him what happened. After all, I wasn't his girlfriend and whenever we got into a fight and left, he didn't follow me. So why follow me now, when we hadn't seen each other in weeks and it was just a dirty fuck?

I'd never seen him worried like that. Especially not over me.

I didn't expect him to search for me when I never went back to the bar; I didn't expect him to be so angry, so hurt, since he never was before. He never came for me ever. And he never yelled at me like that either. Maybe that's why I slammed the door in his face.

I was going through so much, that having the one person I knew I loved scream at me was something I couldn't take.

Time changes a lot of things, but it's never changed the way my heart feels when I think of the look in Madox's eyes that night. When I told him I regretted being with him, and that I wished I hadn't seen him that night. I pushed him away as hard as I could.

I told him I wished I'd never opened my heart to him again, to a man who had no room or need for me in his life. It was my own fault, and I told him so. I'm not sure how much of that is the truth, and how much is a lie.

I was a silly twenty-year-old girl, suffering through life

and running back to my first love every time I felt alone. Since I was seventeen that's what I'd done. Madox Reed was a hard habit to break, but I broke it that night, three years ago.

I imagine he expected me to come back to him, like I always had for the four years I was with him, but I didn't. A very large piece of me loved him for what he'd done for me when we first met, but what we craved from each other only led to pain.

We didn't speak love the same way. He barely spoke it at all, if he ever did.

That was the second time that Madox showed me how he really felt. He didn't hide behind a wall of armor and disinterest.

The first time though, I thought there was a real shift between us. Even if we never spoke about it afterward, I know things changed, for me at least. We'd been seeing each other for only a few months when it happened. Maybe that's why I stayed for four years, even though I never had what I needed to feel truly loved.

He was always in control and private, but on the anniversary of his father's death, Madox came and got me. When he told me his parents had gotten into a fight over the business and his dad killed himself a few years back, I cried for him while he didn't respond. The pain in his eyes was obvious, but he didn't show it. No tears, nothing but the absence of the man I knew he was. He went cold and silent. He told me he needed me to stay with him and I didn't question it for a second, even though I knew something was wrong. It was the only time he told me he needed me like that.

It wasn't until we were in bed that he let his guard down, and he held me just a little tighter while he cried silently. He pretended not to, he said he had no right to be upset when there was so much in his life that other people didn't have. That his father chose to do that and leave him, and at those words, his voice cracked. He tried to get up and leave, but I only hugged him harder, pulling him back into the sheets and against my body, and he let me comfort him.

It didn't matter that he was suffering, because he was so aware that many others had it worse than he did. I remember whispering quietly and gently in between soft kisses on his jaw, that if you're having a bad day, you're entitled to feel those emotions. It's okay to have a bad day even if someone else is having a worse day. It doesn't detract from what you feel inside. If it did, you couldn't be happy for the good times, because someone else always has it better. I told him that it was okay to feel whatever it was he was feeling. That it wasn't wrong to be upset or hurt. I don't know that he believed me though.

That was when I said I loved him. I told him I loved him, and that night he told me the same. Neither of us ever said those words again. Four years went by and I convinced myself that he said it back to me out of obligation. Out of pity.

Just from that memory, the emotions cloud my judgment of today and where we stand now.

I have to remind myself that I when I left three years ago,

I gave Madox the chance to keep me. And he didn't take it. The text message I sent him was marked read. He saw it, and still he let me leave.

He never bothered to show me that he wanted me. Madox Reed couldn't be bothered to show anyone at all that he needed them. It's simply who he is.

"Sophie!" I hear my name and turn in my seat to see the one and only Adrienne Hart walking toward me with a nude leather bag draped over her arm. "It's so wonderful to finally meet you in person."

My fingers wrap around the edge of the chair as I stand up to greet her, but Adrienne keeps moving, not slowing her pace at all to sit across from me at the table.

And here I was wondering if I should give her a hug or a handshake.

She doesn't look me in the eyes as she speaks, slipping off her tweed Chanel jacket. "I trust you found everything you needed last night?" she asks and as I begin to answer, the waiter comes to the table, digging in the black apron hung around his small hips for his pad of paper and pen.

"Just a chai latte, no sweetener," she orders before he says a word, and my lips slam shut so I don't cut her off.

Placing one forearm on the table, and the other on top of the first, Adrienne squares her shoulders, making her slender neck look even longer and letting her platinum blonde bob swing perfectly into place before questioning me, "So... last night?"

I have to clear my throat and give her a fake-ass smile as I say, "It was wonderful. I missed the city." I keep it professional and reach for the goblet of water the waiter left behind for me. There's a dark ring on the black tablecloth from where it sat. The beads of condensation make my hand slip slightly, but she doesn't notice.

"I was going to recommend a bar around the corner to help with the jitters from traveling all day, but I forgot to write you... what is it?" She ponders as I take a sip, and I cough up the small bit of water when she says, "The Tipsy Room."

Fate just wants to fuck with me today.

Luckily, the cruel joke goes unnoticed by Mrs. Hart as she greets two more people, waving them to the table to join us.

This time I stay seated, and this time both of them offer their hands to me. Of course mine is cold and wet from the goblet and I feel the need to apologize awkwardly.

"I'm thrilled to finally meet you; we've heard so much about you," the woman tells me. She's got to be in her late forties or older, judging by the wrinkles around her eyes, but overall she looks so young. If it weren't for the crow's feet, I'd have guessed she wasn't even thirty. *Maybe it's Maybelline, or maybe it's Botox.*

"Lara Bolton." She tells me her name before I have to ask. I had no idea anyone else would be here, and I haven't met anyone other than Adrienne. The second I hear her name, the butterflies in the pit of my belly morph into a hornet's nest. "And this is Hugh North, he'll be training you on all of the technical processes at work starting tomorrow."

"Pleasure," Hugh says with a charming smile. As Lara takes her seat, she hands him her coat and he takes his time removing his navy bomber jacket, which complements his dark skin.

"It's wonderful to meet you both. I've heard," I say and gesture with my hand toward Lara, "everything about you." My pulse ramps up as I think about every article I've read. Lara is a restaurant stylist whose talent is to die for. Her designs aren't just on trend – she *makes* the trends.

"Same to you, Miss Miller," Lara replies with a grin and then the waiter comes to the table, forcing me to be quiet. Which is probably best at the moment.

Before Lara's finished ordering, Hugh places a manila folder and a brand-new laptop in front of me. "Your first assignment."

I'm too eager to wait for anything more, and as I flip through the pages, most of them photographs, Hugh asks me, "What do you think?" There's an air of curiosity from him I find exciting.

I answer quickly, thumbing through the pictures, "This is an easy fix. It's an Irish pub, judging by the name of the restaurant, but there isn't an ounce of green in the branding; no dark woods, the menu is right though—beer-infused cheese dips and all sorts of burgers." When no one says anything, I continue voicing my thoughts aloud.

"The food appears to be on point, but everything else

seems wrong." All their heads nod, and I continue to skim through the pages. It's all white, almost sterile and clinical in appearance, but it's just about getting the aesthetic right. "I could rebrand this place in my sleep."

"Your budget is high too," Hugh says, and I peek up to see all of them grinning at me.

"What about the location?" I ask, not finding it easily in the pamphlet.

"High competition, but if they could draw in the right people, they'd make it work," Lara answers before Hugh can.

"How much time do I have?"

Lara and Hugh share a glance, and Lara offers me a wicked smile. "You're hosting the client meeting tomorrow. But from the sound of your initial assessment, I'm confident you'll have amazing ideas."

Hugh adds as my anxiety spikes, "It's trial by fire here, but I'm sure you'll do just fine with your presentation."

Holy shit. My heart's pounding so fast, it feels like I at least earned *one* of the curtains in my expensive-ass dining room.

With a feigned smile, I let the folder close and tell the table I'll be ready.

Chapter 9

Madox
Seven Years Ago

I think she's going to say it again, but she doesn't.

Instead, she offers me a small smile and I force one back.

I've been waiting to hear those words again, but she hasn't said them since that one time. I thought it would bring us closer, but all I can feel is distance. I should have known better than to lean on her like I did. I should have been on my own. I should have dealt with it myself.

She said it to make me feel better. That's all.

"You okay?" she asks me.

"Fine." My answer is stern. I am fine. I'm her rock. I'll keep being her rock. That's what she needs. That's what I'll be.

Today

Everyone wants something. It's fucking constant.

If I had nothing, no one would message me. My inbox would be empty. No one would have to wait for an appointment to sit in the chair across from me.

I know it's true, because I was there at one point when I took over this failing company and worked tirelessly to bring it back to its former glory and then surpass it. I was only fifteen when my dad died, and eighteen when my mother shoved me into this role. I learned young that nothing comes without a price.

The patter of rain has been a constant all day, hitting the glass wall behind me and lulling me into a false sense of peace.

I keep staring at my phone, noting how only ten minutes pass each time I check. I'm waiting for a text, or an email… something from Sophie. As if she has any reason to want a damn thing from me.

Of everyone who desires a piece of me, or something I have to offer, I just want one of them to be her.

The rap of knuckles at my door breaks my thoughts of what used to be, and I'm grateful for it. Until it opens before I can answer, and Ryan strides into the room.

"So?" Ryan's smirk is cocky and confident as he settles into the seat across from me, tapping the tips of his fingers, eagerly waiting for details.

"So, what?" I fuck with him, keeping my own smirk in check. "Did you get your notice?"

"Notice?" he asks, and the smirk fades as his lips droop down.

"You're fucking fired for two reasons." I keep my voice hard as I lean forward and tell him, "One: You put your manwhore hands on Sophie the other night. Two: You knew she was here, and you didn't tell me."

"Oh fuck off, I only knew she was there for a minute more than you. Come on and tell me what happened." Ryan brushes me off, but I don't budge. He can suffer for a moment like I did. The exasperated sigh that leaves him is what gets me to show a little humor.

"Tell me what happened," he presses.

"Lunch with my mother was awful, thanks for asking."

"That was a given." Ryan disregards my comment and leans forward to ask, "You and baby girl back to normal?"

No. I know the answer, and simply shake my head, feeling the deadweight sit against my chest as I turn off my computer. I still have hours before dinner, but I'd rather distract myself with Ryan and anything other than work before meeting Sophie tonight.

"We hit it off just like normal, but she's not ..." The back of my throat goes dry, so I pick up my coffee, drinking it black as always.

"She still loves you," he tells me gently as if that's what the problem ever was.

"She's resistant to being with me." I finally settle on that truth, spacing out the words and letting them sit in the air while Ryan considers them.

He slumps back, letting his back hit the chair and turns his hands up as he says, "She always has been resistant, hasn't she?" When I don't answer he adds, "You didn't think she'd just fall into bed with you and go right back to being what it used to be, did you?"

"You're the one who said 'normal,'" I remind him, barely hiding my irritation. He's never had a stable relationship. He doesn't mind living vicariously through the only one I've ever wanted. She doesn't want it to be what it used to be. I can't tell him that part. I'm ashamed of it. I thought it was good. How could I have been so wrong? I thought I was good for her. I thought I was good *to* her.

"See, I thought you had a stick up your ass the last few years because you hadn't gotten your dick wet, but here we are, and that stick hasn't budged."

"How'd you know?"

"That you guys fucked?" he asks me with a brow cocked and his forehead scrunched. As if it's an odd question to ask. I just gaze at him coolly and he shrugs.

"She told Trish, who told Brett, who told me about ten

minutes ago."

"Word travels fast."

Ryan shrugs unapologetically. "It's been a long time coming... So you got her in bed... and then what?"

"That's none of anyone's business."

"Aw, come on, Brett and Trish only know so much. You've got to give me something." Brett and Trish know too damn much. Trish I can understand, although I'm still pissed she didn't tell me Sophie was coming back. And Brett needs to mind his own fucking business.

"Can we talk about something else?" I ask, not hiding the irritation in my voice.

"So your lunch date with your mom went poorly?"

I grin at him as I reply, "I hate you."

"You love me so much. I could feel the waves of adoration from all the way down the hall to my office."

"You should have stayed there and finished the numbers for the meeting tomorrow."

"Already done," he tells me and I'm quick to retort, "For the meeting Friday then."

He only snorts a laugh and there's a moment of awkward silence. The kind that comes when someone's begging to ask you a question, but they don't know how you'll react.

I tell him, "Just say it. Whatever it is."

"What did your mom want?" he asks me with nervous hesitation. My mother is never a topic of pleasant conversation.

"To tell me she's getting another divorce."

"I thought she just married ...Steve?"

"She divorced Stewart last year, this one's name is Jerry." Although the conversation is almost casual in tone, it's anything but.

"Ah." Ryan nods and raises his brow as high as he can before sucking in air through his teeth. "Well, maybe the next one will be a winner."

"Doubtful," I mutter under my breath and stand abruptly, ending the conversation. My mother wouldn't know love if it sent her the biggest paycheck she'd ever seen.

Chapter 10

Sophie
Six Years Ago

"**H**ey." *Madox's voice is gentle as he approaches.* "You fell asleep out here," *he tells me as if I didn't intend to sleep out on the sofa. He wouldn't talk to me. Wasn't he mad at me?*

"Oh," *I say like I'm surprised, pretending like it was an accident.* "Are you done working?" *I'm hesitant to ask. Lately he's been working extra hours a lot and half the time I think he's doing it just to avoid me, the other half of the time I feel like I should be working harder. As hard as he is. It's constant. I'll go to college this fall though and then maybe I'll be just as busy as he is.*

"Come to bed," *he tells me and I do. His thumb rubs soothing circles on my knuckles as we walk hand in hand. I keep looking up at him, not knowing if it's all in my head or not.*

Before climbing into bed, I ask him, "I thought you might be mad at me. I thought maybe I should go home."

"If you want to leave, I'm not going to stop you," he tells me and he says it easily, like the words shouldn't cut so deeply into me. When my parents fought it was with sharp tongues. All it took for Madox to bring me to the point of leaving, was the truth, casually spoken.

He tells me he doesn't know why I'm crying. I swear we speak different languages.

Today

Madox was always good at wining and dining me. At spoiling me with pretty things. That's how he apologized. It's how he said thank you. He spoke with gifts.

Trish told me it's one of the ways to express love. She got it from some book about there being five different love languages. Even if gifts are one way to demonstrate love, it never felt right. Not to me.

He could have bought my entire world a million times over. And all I did was run to him, spread my legs and stay in his bed instead of going home. It felt like... it felt like he was buying me. I didn't want his gifts.

I told him that once. It didn't end well. One of our many

breakups.

When we got back together, he told me the Tiffany necklace he put around my neck was from a dollar store. So it didn't count as "buying my affection."

I can't explain how powerless I felt in that moment, but also how cherished. I still have that necklace. I love that necklace.

I'm trying not to feel the same way now as I take my seat in the private room in the back of The Cherie. It's a fresh start and new beginnings. I'm not the same girl I was back then, and this isn't "buying" me. It's just dinner.

Maybe it's a way for him to show me he loves me, as Trish would say. I asked her what my love language was and she said words of affirmation. That I like to be told things, told that I'm pretty, that I'm doing well, told that I'm loved. I laughed when she said it and told her, "No wonder it didn't work between us. I couldn't afford to tell him I loved him and he couldn't speak it."

Inside the restaurant is exactly as fancy as I pictured in my head. White linens and polished marble walls. It's the kind of restaurant where not a single expense is spared, and the waiters wear cuff links and spit-shined black shoes.

"Thank you," I tell said waiter, and try not to pull down the skirt of my dress as he pours water into our glasses. I don't touch my hem until he's turned his back and no one can see me squirm... except for Madox. Like always, I'm not quite dressed for the occasion.

It feels like our first date all over again. Where he knows all the tricks and holds all the cards, and I'm barely gripping on to anything.

"Dark blue is your color." Madox's words make my heart do that stuttering thing. I can feel heat flood up my chest and to my cheeks. With a soft smirk kicking up the corners of his lips he adds, "Blushing looks good on you too."

Slipping a lock of hair behind my ear, I tell him, "Thank you. You look handsome too... you always do."

The fluttering in my chest matches the way my stomach feels, and I search around the stark white tabletop for a menu of any kind. For anything at all to distract me from the sincerity of Madox's gaze. But there's nothing save polished silverware and lit candles.

"I like it when you do that," he says lowly, in a tone that hits straight to my core. I have to lift my eyes to his, barely able to breathe at seeing the look in his eyes.

"Do what?"

"Compliment me."

"I'm sure you have lots of people do that." Even as I speak without conscious consent, I can't help but to look over every bit of his features and feel a pinch in my brow.

"They're not you."

"That's very sweet of you."

"It's also true. I'm glad you agreed to come out tonight."

"You're different, Madox," I barely whisper and wish I had

a menu or something to hold in my hands. Instead, I shove them into my lap and wring my fingers around one another as Madox, with a look of slight vulnerability on his handsome face, asks me how. He stays perfectly still though, never showing anything more than a glimpse that he may be less than in control.

"It's just ..." I bite down on my bottom lip and try to put it into words. "When I remember us, you didn't talk much about," I pause as I struggle to come up with an explanation. "About anything, really. I never knew what you were thinking about back then."

"Trish told me you prefer words of affirmation," Madox tells me as he takes the beautifully folded napkin in front of him and lays it on his lap. "She told me we need to learn each other's forms of communication, and I'm trying. I think she may have insight I lacked when we were together."

Madox's features could be carved of marble. They're flawless and classically handsome; perfectly poised. My own feel like they're crumbling at what he just told me. It's a pain, but a good one. Like when you've given yourself to someone for the first time, and the powerful mix of emotions surges inside of you, looking for a way out—until they kiss you, hold you close. That's the kind of pain I feel right now. Along with the panic of being too vulnerable.

"You're too far away from me," Madox tells me, cutting off my thoughts.

I have to grin at his statement. We're alone in the room and I can only imagine what he'd do to me if we were closer. The very thought makes me squirm, and I can tell from the look in his eyes he would do whatever the hell he wanted with me back here.

"Do you remember when I ate you out under the table at ... what was that place?" he asks me and my core heats immediately, remembering how he didn't give me any notice, he simply ducked down under the table in the middle of the restaurant and slipped his hands up my skirt. All while I stared fixedly at the wall, trying not to scream in pleasure.

"Blue Hill."

"Yes," he says and nods, picking up his drink then adds, "you loved that place. How could I forget?" My heart flutters in a way that wishes I were closer to him right now. As close as I could be, but instead I stare down at the silverware, which makes my smile come back.

I was sure someone was looking at me when my silverware hit the plate of the chocolate lava cake with a loud clatter that night he crawled under the table at Blue Hill.

"My hand shook when I tried to drink my water, you know? It was hard to play it off."

He flashes a wolfish grin back at me. "It was the day before your birthday, I remember that."

"Is that why you did it? An early birthday present?"

He shakes his head once, a short and deliberate no. "I did

it because I wanted to taste you right then and there." My nipples pebble and my pussy clenches, instantly remembering how his tongue dove into me, how his fingers gripped my hips.

My voice is merely a murmur when I tell him, "You do always get what you want, don't you?"

"Right now, I want to fuck you on this table. So you tell me, Sophie."

My heart slams, the heat rising and flooding every inch of my body.

The nerves intensify until Madox nods his head toward someone over my shoulder.

"I sent in the order on my way here," Madox says and waits for my reaction until I nod in understanding, peeking at the waiter as he makes his way over with our first dishes.

Right now, I wish I had something to give Madox. A gift of some kind. I don't know what I could give a man like him, someone who has everything. I want to try too though. If he's trying, I'm going to try with everything I have.

The young man is professional as he sets our food down in front of us. Bone white china plates with a fennel and leek citrus salad beautifully arranged on the dishes. As the waiter explains the first course, a silent lady in black dress pants and a gorgeous white blouse pours the paired wine, some Chenin Blanc.

It's all beautiful and decadent, but I couldn't name half the ingredients if someone told me they'd pay me a million dollars cash right now to tell me what I was eating.

Once we're alone again, I thank Madox and change the subject to something that isn't going to get me fucked on this table. "I like it when you order in advance, although then I can't hide behind the menu." With a flirtatious smile, I take a bite and savor the sweetness of the expensive dinner.

He smirks at me as if he knows exactly what I'm doing. And he goes with it. Giving me a moment to breathe and come down from the high I was just on, remembering what this man across from me is capable of.

There's tension between us, but it's the good kind.

"Good, isn't it?" Madox asks, lifting the glass of wine to his lips, but not drinking until I answer him. I have to cover my mouth and finish swallowing when he smiles at me like that. Because when he does, I smile too.

He chuckles into his glass when I nod, and as he sips I tell him it's all delicious.

"The lobster risotto is next. I think that will be your favorite."

Letting my fingers slip down the stem of the glass I ask him, "Will there be another glass as well?" and he nods. *Shit*. These places always give you so much wine and so little food.

"I have to work tonight," I tell him, voicing the concern that's keeping me on edge.

The light in Madox's eyes, that fire dims slightly, but it's back just as quickly as it left. "I could have it all wrapped up to go if you'd prefer."

"No, no, I just can't drink ...much." Lifting the glass to my lips and deciding this will be my only glass until the presentation is done tonight, I tell Madox offhandedly, "I'm a little too carefree when I drink."

"What's wrong with being carefree?" he questions, although it's meant to be playful.

"Well, last night for one," I answer him honestly. It's not healthy to do what we do. "I probably shouldn't have slept with you." An anxiousness comes over me, this feeling of dread.

"Why is that?" he asks, sitting up straighter and placing his hands on the table. His fingers are interlaced as his thumbs roll over one another. I imagine this is how he looks at business meetings. Intimidating.

"Well that makes me kind of easy, doesn't it?"

"I wouldn't use the word 'easy.' You've never been easy to hold on to."

I start to say it would have been better between the two of us back then if he'd been open with me like this, but it feels like the start of a fight and that's the last thing I want.

Habits are hard to break and when I left three years ago, I spent a lot of time with self-help books. Lord knows I needed it. I'm trying to break the habit of picking fights with him. Toward the end, I think I'd pick a fight just to see if he would ever tell me to stay.

He never did.

I already wish I hadn't brought up this topic. It's begging

to be spoken from the tip of my tongue though. I want to know what he wants. For years I've wanted to know what I mean to him.

It feels so obvious to me right now, but is it so wrong that I want to hear it? And even worse, that I'm afraid of what he'll say.

"Thank you for inviting me out. I needed it after today," I say to change the subject, feeling a cowardly chill run down my spine at the mere idea that Madox will tell me I'm an old friend, or friend with benefits, or something like that if I were to ask him.

"What's wrong?"

"Just a lot of stress at work."

"I wish you wouldn't lie to me." Madox's gaze leaves me and it feels like a punishment. I can feel his disappointment. That's how much power and control this man has over me. I hate disappointing him.

"I don't know that I want to talk about it," I answer hesitantly. "I don't want to upset you."

Madox considers me for a moment, his forehead marred by a deep crease and his dark green eyes swimming with questions.

"I respect that," he tells me with sincerity. His voice is low though, as if he hates to allow me that freedom of not confiding in him.

He changes the subject, but to something I didn't expect.

"I saw my mother today."

"Oh?" I ask him, glancing just for a moment to the waiter who's suddenly at my side, offering him a small smile he doesn't see as he clears the table of the porcelain plates.

Madox finishes his thought only once we're alone again. "So I had a rough day as well."

"How is she?" I ask. "Is it still the way it was?"

"The two of us not speaking and pretending there's anything at all we could talk about? Yes. It's exactly like that." He may not realize it, but every time he speaks about his mother, there's anger in his tone. Coupled with an impatience I don't see from him often.

"I'm sorry to hear that," I say, and my words are calm and gentle, as is my hand reaching out to him. He accepts my offer, lacing his fingers between mine.

It feels so good to touch him. I have to close my eyes for a moment to remind myself that this is real. He's really here and he's even talking to me about his mother.

Maybe I'm not the only one who read some self-help books after I left.

"Don't be," he tells me as his thumb rubs circles along my wrist. "We haven't had a relationship since my father..." Madox doesn't finish that sentence, but then he adds, "And I doubt we ever will."

"Even if it feels like you have everything, it's okay to be upset about the things you don't have. You know that, right?"

His eyes flash to mine with an intense heat, and he stares

at me as if what I've said is foolish. "I do. I'm well aware of that ... even as I sit across the table from you right now."

It hadn't occurred to me that my words could be used against me, which is exactly what this feels like. My hand slips from his grasp, and he allows it. I drag it back to my lap.

"What's holding you back?" Madox asks me.

"Back from what?"

"Your guard is up. Not just a little. I can barely see you. The real you."

I clear my throat and try to meet his eyes so I can be honest about how I'm feeling, but I can't even do that. "You intimidate me," is all I manage to get out.

"I'll listen to whatever you tell me. Just talk to me," he says, and his voice holds an edge of desperation. It's something I've never heard from him. Not like this.

Staring down at the barren white tablecloth, I speak, letting it all come out.

It's a real conversation. That's what this is. Our first real conversation. Probably ever. It's so much easier to allow fears to be unspoken.

"I've only just come back to New York, days ago. I don't have a grip on anything at all in my life right now. I feel an immense amount of pressure. I'm worried and excited at the same time. I'm happy..." With that admission, I can look him in the eyes as I continue, "For the first time in a really long while." My throat gets tight and tears prick at the back of my eyes, but I hold them back. "And I'm afraid that I'm going to be swept up by you, and I'm going to lose this part of me that's actively working to choose happiness and create a stable income. More than that, I'm afraid this isn't going to last and I'm going to let myself fall, only to be shattered at a time in my life where I can't afford that."

I can barely breathe, waiting for Madox to say anything at all. A moment passes, more dishes are placed in front of us – although there's no way I could possibly eat a damn thing right now – and it's not until the doors behind us close again, leaving us to ourselves that Madox asks me, "You didn't plan on coming back to see me then?"

It fucking hurts to see the pain etched in his expression right now.

"I didn't know... I haven't spoken to you in so long. ... Trish never told me that you messaged until today. When I told her I saw you, she told me you asked about me. I didn't know you were thinking about me. I would have never thought you'd make an effort like you are right now, because it never felt like you did back then."

It's awkward; laying everything out on the table feels like willingly drowning yourself. "I feel," I have to swallow before adding, "If I had known..." My head is teeming with thoughts and I can barely focus on a single one. For three years I rehearsed every conversation in my head I wanted to have with this man, and in all of them, he never cared. So to sit here and see how much he does... I'm struggling. It's all too much, and I can feel myself slipping backward.

I refuse to go back to who I used to be.

"Would it have made a difference?" Madox asks in a low tone, pushing his plate to the side and bringing his hand to rest on top of mine.

"Would what have?" I ask him, feeling a wave of emotional exhaustion. I love this man. That was never a question. And that's what makes it hurt the most. Even after all these years I still love him. I loved him back then and it wasn't enough though. Love isn't always enough.

"If you'd known that I was asking about you, would you have come back for me?"

"Not at first, no. I was scared and I needed to find myself after what happened with my parents that week."

"Did you?"

"Yes."

He doesn't hesitate to ask me another question, and I don't hesitate to answer.

"Did you miss me?"

"Of course I did. You have no idea." My voice is choked when I tell him, "Some days just to feel okay, I would pretend you were holding me." I remember what it felt like back then, to be so alone in the spare room of Trish's apartment, crying on the bed. Letting every bit of me break. I knew if I went back, Madox would hold me and take away the pain. But then he'd eventually let me go, and I wouldn't know what to do with myself because the only identity I had was to be his. His burden.

I want to brush the tear from my eye before it can fall, but I refuse to let go of his hands right now. Not with the way his warm touch reminds me how life has changed, and I'm not in the same position I once was. At least I can stand on my own now. This is the first time I can sit in front of him and say that much.

"I remember what you said the night before you left when I found you at your place... about being more than a dirty fuck," Madox starts to speak after a moment of silence.

I cut him off before he can continue. "I don't think I meant half of what I said, Madox." I feel awful inside, desperately wanting to avoid going back to that night and how everything happened. I don't want to go back. It hurts too much. I can't go back.

"It meant something though. Even in our lies there's some truth, and it took me a while to understand why you said that. It was never just sex with you, Soph. You felt that way, didn't you? You thought I only wanted you for sex?" I can only nod, admitting how little I thought of myself back then. I was willing to stay with him, hoping one day he'd want more. Hoping one day he'd realize how much I loved him and tell me that I was worth loving back. Worth loving even when I wasn't in bed with him.

Every night I've been alone taunts me in this moment. Seeing how much he cares, when for years I convinced myself he didn't, all so I could learn to get better on my own.

"Why didn't you--" I want to ask him about the text he never answered before I took off as I pull my hands away, grabbing my napkin and wiping away the tears as delicately as I can, but I can't finish my sentence.

Another minute passes and the energy in the air becomes suffocating until Madox speaks.

"I didn't have to run away to figure out who I was. I know who I am, and I don't like that person without you."

It fucking kills me to hear him say that. I can't stand to hear him say that.

"Madox," I cry his name. I'm doing my best to hold it together, but it's fucking impossible. There's no armor left to hide behind and without it, I can't even breathe.

"My biggest regret though... is that I wish I'd talked to Brett before seeing you that night. He knew what happened to your parents and if I'd known, that night wouldn't have happened the way it did. I would have been better for you. I didn't know they'd died. If I'd known about the accident, I wouldn't have taken you out back to the alley, thinking that's what you wanted. I would have been able to keep you if I'd known. I wouldn't have messed up."

The mention of my parents breaks me. Of my mom and how she died in a car accident. She'd texted me earlier that day and I ignored her. She told me she loved me, and I didn't respond. I got so used to not saying it back. Hours later, a car went through a red light and both my mom and stepdad were killed instantly. I was never able to tell her I loved her again. Even if our relationship was strained, I did love her.

Regret is a horrible way to live. He may hate who he was without me. I hated who I was with him. I hated what I was and I never want to be that girl again.

What's worse is that I know he's right when he says he still would have had me if he'd known. That splinters the already broken pieces of my heart.

"I can't." I barely breathe the words, shoving away from the table as my shoulders shake.

"I have to go, Madox." I try to utter an apology as I stand on shaky legs.

"Let me-"

"No," I say and push him away. "No, Madox. I need to be alone. I need to be okay with being alone. Please, please. I need to be alone right now."

He tries to follow me and I beg him, just for a moment. I tell him I'm not leaving him; I'm just leaving this moment. I reminded him I had to work and that it was important to me. I promised him that I'd call him and see him again. That's what allows him to let me go back to the apartment that's not mine and calm myself down before I can work.

I just hope I don't break my promise.

Chapter 11

Madox
Four Years Ago

"Is it enough if I say I'm sorry?" I ask her. She keeps running off, burying herself in schoolwork and her internship. I understand that, but she's staying at her parents' apartment instead of here with me. She lies and says it's because their place is closer to the university. I know that's not why; I just don't know what I did.

"Are you sorry?" she asks me and I tell her I am; even though I don't know what I did. There's something about me that pushes her away and I don't know what it is, but perhaps it's just me. I'm damned to watch her leave me. Maybe that's the way it's supposed to be for me.

I know I'm supposed to be with her; that is the only reason I could feel this way when I'm with her, this need to be close to her. I *think she's damned to run away and I'm damned to watch her run.*

I'll be okay with that though, as long as we get to hold each other after.

"Then come to bed," I tell her and she follows. She runs but she always comes back. As long as she comes back, it's fine. Even though I know it's not fine, I tell myself it is because that's better than knowing one day, she isn't going to come back.

TODAY

Give her time. Trish's advice is the same as Brett's. It's the same as Ryan's. Everyone keeps telling me to give her time. Don't they know, time doesn't heal pain? She needs someone to take it away.

I can be that someone.

I've waited three years. I can wait another day, another week. However long it takes.

If she doesn't want me because she wants to be okay being alone—I don't know that she'll ever come back to me. Why would she? We were so damaged toward the end, it hurts just to think about.

I fucked up, and I don't know how to make things right. For the first time in a long time, I don't know what to do.

Sitting on the edge of my bed, I think back on every moment

I could have changed what was bound to happen. Every time she cried softly and I held her, but I didn't ask why she was so upset. Holding her seemed to be enough and I didn't trust my words. I thought holding her would be enough.

It's my fault she doesn't love me enough to stay. That's what it comes down to. I don't know how to make her love me any more than she does.

She does love me. But it's not enough.

My phone buzzes on the nightstand, and keeps going.

Someone's calling, probably Cody, if someone's told him Sophie's back. Or Brett or Ryan, if they heard about tonight. As much as I'm grateful they give a damn, they can all fuck off.

They told me to wait for her before, and it didn't fucking work.

Without looking at the ID, I answer it to say, "I'm not going out; I don't give a shit if you tell me I'm being a bitch or not. It's not happening."

There's hesitation on the end of the line until I hear my mother's voice coolly reply, "I would never call you *a bitch*, for starters."

Fuck, I think and my eyes roll back into my head with irritation. As if my night couldn't get any worse.

"Mother," I talk over her. "I wasn't expecting you. It's late."

"I wanted to see if you'd gotten the message about the dinner?" she asks me, her voice returning to the normal proper state. The kind of proper that requires a stick up your ass.

"I received your message, yes." I don't bother telling her I'm not going. She should already know that. Considering she didn't bring it up at lunch, I'm sure she's well aware I have no intention of attending.

My mother starts to speak and then stops herself. I can hear that she's still there, although it's silent for a moment. "I heard that something happened at The Cherie tonight, and so I was also calling because I wanted to make sure you were alright."

Whoever spoke a word to her is going to be fired. There's no fucking way any of my friends would go to my mother. Maybe it was the waiter, or maybe the fucking chef. I don't know who, but I'm going to find out and make their life a living hell. I pay good fucking money for privacy.

"Tell me something, please." My mother's voice actually carries a maternal note to it when she adds, "I'm your mother."

She wants to know? As if she couldn't put two and two together.

"I fell in love with a girl a long time ago and I couldn't show her." I harden my voice to add, "I don't know how. I never learned."

I can hear her swallow. "Well how is it that you're treating her? I may have some ideas of what you could do," she offers and it's nearly comical. She adds in a self-deprecating tone, "I've been married three times, you know. I could tell you why I said yes each time."

Her sad laugh is weak on the other end of the line, and

I feel for her. I mourn for my mother, both what she went through and for the woman she decided to be.

"I know I've made many mistakes, Madox, but if I can just listen, I would be grateful right now."

I don't answer her. Instead, I remember the one time I saw her cry in my life because I think I can hear her crying now. "I'll be quiet and just listen." Her voice cracks and she sniffles before adding, "You can pretend I'm not even here."

"I don't want to upset you," I tell her in a single breath, feeling like a prick and hating myself even more. A deep-rooted painful side of me wants to add, *I didn't think it was possible*, but I don't. I won't hurt her when she's already suffering.

"I'm sorry," I tell her, and she tries to hide the pain when she says in croaked words, "Just tell me what happened."

A moment passes before I pretend I'm not talking to her. I'm just trying to piece together the frayed edges of what I had with Sophie.

"I liked being the one who could take her pain away and I thought it was enough to show her I loved her." The ceiling fan continues to spin as I stare up at it and I continue to talk. "But she doesn't want me to be that for her anymore. And I don't know what I can be to her, if she doesn't want to ..." Fuck, it hurts. Pinching the bridge of my nose, I try to push it down.

I won't let her walk away. I'll keep her.

I will.

There is no other possibility.

"Have you tried telling her that you hurt? Maybe she would feel better leaning on you, if you leaned some on her." My mother's words are met with silence.

That isn't fair to Sophie. The weight of my pain isn't fair to put on anyone, let alone the girl I love. My mother continues speaking when I don't say anything.

"It could just be you're upset that she doesn't feel she can..." she pauses, maybe figuring out the words to use as she finishes, "lean on you while also being her own person." Her voice picks up, carrying optimism with her words. "Even something as little as that could maybe make a difference. Maybe?"

It's an odd feeling when a sad smile pulls at my lips. It's half assed and defeated, but I feel it.

"Thank you, mother," is all I give her, but it's more than I have in a long time. It's genuine.

"Will you please come to dinner?" she asks me without wasting a second, going right back to her like she always does, but this time I tell her, "Yes. I'll be there."

It was nice to pretend I still have a relationship with her and that she didn't fuck me over entirely.

Chapter 12

Sophie
Four Years Ago

"Hey," *Madox says and it scares the shit out of me. The sight of him in the cafeteria is ... odd. He doesn't belong at a small folding table outside of the sub shop and surrounded by kids younger than him in PJs and jeans.*

"Hey," *I answer him and move my tray down the table.* "What are you doing here?"

"I didn't see you last night," *he answers as if that would be obvious.*

"I've been staying in the library a lot and I crashed hard when I got in. I went to the office." *My skin pricks when I tell him that, the kind of prick that feels poisonous and hurts you deep down inside. He's going to end it with me any day now. He'll tell me to just stop coming around at all. I know he will. I think he's been wanting that for a long time, but he doesn't want to be that cruel. He's waiting for me to leave for good. Maybe that's why he's here.*

He just keeps looking down at me, rather than sitting. "Do you want an apple?" I offer him, simply to break up the silence.

"You're giving me an apple?"

"I have half a sandwich too," I add, wondering if he's eaten as he sits down next to me. I wish I had more to give him.

"I can go get something for you?" I offer him but he shakes his head. He doesn't bite the apple, but he holds it in both hands, letting his thumb run down the shiny red skin when he tells me, "I know you're working a lot, and I love that you've found what you're passionate about. I like it when you come to bed though, even if it's late."

"I can do that," I answer him quickly, happy that he still wants me. When he leaves, I hate the realization that there's nothing at all that makes me as happy as hearing him tell me he wants me. I know it's not good. I'm not good. We're not good. But I keep holding on because I want him to be happy too.

Today

It's well past time to leave work, but I'm not ready to go back to that apartment yet. I don't want to go back to it at all.

I'm already finished with the mock-ups for all three clients this week.

I can't do anything with them until Lara approves. She gave me the entire week to prepare them, but I feel like I'm deep down at the bottom of a black hole after the meeting today. Six hours straight without even moving from my desk. I'll look them over tomorrow before sending them to Lara, but I can feel it in my bones that they're exactly what the clients need and want.

I have no reason to stay any longer, but still, I head for Adrienne's office in the back right corner, feeling the heaviness in my eyes as I do.

I didn't sleep last night. Not at all. The presentation went off without a hitch, but only because coffee and concealer exist. I don't think anyone can tell that I am barely hanging on by a thread.

Hesitating only to smooth my skirt, I finally knock on Adrienne's door. She's still here along with a few others in the cubicles, but this entire floor is nearly empty.

"Who is it?" she calls out.

Shit. It's awkward speaking through the wood door, but I do. "Sophie Miller. I just wanted a quick word."

Embarrassment floods my face, all the way up to my temples, but she tells me to come in and I suck in a breath, knowing I should be quick. I don't know what I was thinking coming unannounced.

You were thinking: I don't want to go home.

My mouth is open before the door is even closed, ready to tell her I only wanted to thank her for giving me the opportunity and I hope the presentation was everything they expected, but my lips slam shut.

Adrienne's face is red, her cheeks tearstained. She smiles brightly anyway, not bothering to hide the fact that she must have been crying.

"I'm so sorry, I can come back another time," I murmur and reach behind me for the doorknob, feeling like a fucking asshole, but Adrienne tells me to stay.

"Your presentation was wonderful. I know Lara was impressed." Her tone is muted, her energy drained.

"Thank you. That's what I..." I pause and step forward, and she motions for me to sit. I shake my head and tell her, "I just wanted to thank you. That's all. I really appreciate you giving me a chance, and I'm so happy it went well today." I don't even know what words just came out of my mouth because I'm so distracted by how distraught Adrienne is. And how she's pretending like she isn't.

"I'm thrilled to hear that," she says politely and nods.

I nod back and feel awkward about it. "I'll go now," I tell her but as I turn, she explains, "I'm getting a divorce and apparently I'm more upset about it than I realized."

Slowly, I turn back to her, a sharp agony piercing through me from her confession. "I'm so sorry." My words are sincere, and I hope she can feel that. "If there's anything I can do," I start to offer, but I can't imagine what that would be.

"It's not your fault, dear, no reason to be sorry. I'll be fine. I shouldn't have put all that on you." Adrienne lifts her bag onto her chair and pulls out a mirror, setting it on her desk.

"It's okay to walk away if it's not right," I offer the woman who obviously knows more than me about life, mostly to comfort her, but I feel ridiculous. What would I know about marriage? Let alone divorce. I simply feel bad for her.

Adrienne gives me a sad smile and says, "It's not really okay. I find myself running away from everything and I really want to run toward something, but my something isn't here anymore." Her voice gets tight and just as I reach out to her, she shakes it off, backing away and leaving me with my hand in the air.

I let it fall slowly as she wipes haphazardly under her eyes and forces her demeanor back to what I've known it to be. "You got the invitation for the client dinner, correct?"

I start to answer, but my throat is dry and I have to clear it before I answer her, "Tomorrow night?"

"Yes, it's going to be lovely. Certainly dress to impress, dear." She glances at me and then adds, "After all, we are the best of the best." Adrienne faces the mirror, tidying up her makeup and I shift uneasily where I stand.

"I'll see you tomorrow then," I tell her, turning toward the door. She only nods, looking down for a moment before looking back in the mirror and bringing her Dior lipstick to her thin lips.

There's a hollowness that follows me as I walk away.

I never thought about life the way she worded it. I was always running away, but I never looked up to see what I was running toward.

Chapter 13

Madox
Four Years Ago

It used to be that she'd stay away for days. But if I texted her to come, she would.

Then those days turned into weeks. And then she was busy.

She's not busy with someone else; it's just work. When I do see her though, the fire that burns between us always comes back. I guess it worked the first few years because she didn't have anything else. I know we're both damaged in a way where we hurt each other, but we make each other feel better too. There's no one who makes me feel better. No one but her.

"Come to dinner tonight. Six o'clock at Blue Hill," I tell her when she answers my call. She loves that place. We have good memories there. That can only be a good thing.

"I wish you'd ask me," she says quietly.

"Will you come to Blue Hill with me?" I ask her, knowing I shouldn't, because recently whenever she's been given the choice she's chosen not to come be with me.

"We have good memories there," she says rather than answering if she'll come with me or not.

"We do."

"I miss those times" she tells me and I don't say anything back. Missing them means they're gone and I can't let that happen. I'll make tonight good for her and then she'll stay. I know she will. She can't hide that she still loves me.

Today

The office is quiet. The sky behind me is black, and the streets beneath me are lit with the traffic of the busy city. So many people, so close.

But I feel so damn alone.

She's been avoiding me. No call last night like she said she would. She didn't answer my texts. She didn't answer my calls today, and Trish isn't giving Brett any details. She isn't giving me much to go on either. She told me Sophie hasn't told her anything other than that she cried when she left the restaurant.

Which made me feel even worse than I already did. As if

some part of me actually thought she wasn't crying alone and refusing to let me comfort her.

The only reason I'm not banging on the door to the address Trish gave me is because Sophie sent a message earlier today asking if we could meet here, at my office.

Don't sweat it. Brett's text hits my phone and I want to throw it across the room. Everyone knows she's avoiding me just like she did back then.

She just needs a little time. Trish's text comes through next and I'm so pissed Brett added her to our chat I nearly throw the phone. *Make sure you tell her you love her.*

What if it's a test? Ryan sends in the group text thread.

Like she's baiting him to see if he'll go get her? he sends another text.

Trish answers him, *She wouldn't do that. Knock it off, Ryan.*

You women do stupid shit, Ryan writes back, making my phone ping again. I put it on silent, but not before I see Trish write him back. *Fuck off.*

They can all shut the hell up and stay out of it. They aren't helping the situation.

Even though the phone's now on silent, I monitor it and the clock both, waiting for Sophie to either message or simply knock on the door.

And just like that, a timid knock reverberates and I call her in. I see her hair first, the long dirty blonde locks covering her face. She brushes it out of the way and when she does, she looks back at me with a pained expression.

"Hey," she tells me softly, watching the door as it closes before taking another small step toward me.

I recognize the tone in her voice, the too-afraid-to-voice-what-needs-to-be-said tone. My heart sinks, and I can feel it drop into the pit of my stomach. With my blood running cold she asks if she can sit down, holding her purse with both of her hands.

I can't speak, I can only focus on not letting what I'm feeling show as I gesture to the plush wingback chair on the opposite side of the desk.

"How are you?" she asks and then swallows, setting her purse down on the floor. I watch her and wait for her eyes to reach mine again before answering honestly. "Not well."

Her lips tug down and her eyes fall.

Fuck, this hurts. I want it to stop. It's not supposed to happen like this.

"Madox. I need to say something... It just feels like it's too much getting back together so quickly, if that's what we're doing. I need a little bit of time to get a grip on things."

I listen carefully. To every word.

"More time," I say out loud, not looking her in the eyes and instead lifting my gaze to the clock. Every minute—every second—without her is hell. How can she want more of this, when I can't stand it?

"I'm not over what happened, and I don't know how to

handle this."

"Over what?" I question her, feeling my anger rise.

"I'm not over that night and how we left things. I can't pretend like it didn't happen."

"Then don't." My voice raises slightly and I have to concentrate to keep it even as I add, "Don't pretend, talk it out with me."

She clenches her mouth shut and breathes out heavily from her nose, looking past me at the darkened sky.

"What specifically aren't you over? What did I do that was so bad that you can't move past it?" The images of that night three years ago come back to me. The way she writhed under me; fuck, she sought me out. She *wanted* me. She came back to me, and I gave her everything I had.

"You mean after you fucked me and called me your whore?" she asks, although I can hear the trace of lust on her lips. "Or maybe you mean when you came into my apartment yelling at me, screaming about how you were so worried--"

"Don't minimize the way I feel," I cut her off, my voice dangerously low as my lungs seize inside of me. She was supposed to come into the bar after me so everyone wouldn't know we just fucked after being apart for almost a month. She said she'd straighten up, so I should go in first. But she never came. Fifteen minutes passed before I banged on the door to the women's bathroom, finding it empty except for some brunette who looked pissed off until she saw me.

"If you're angry I raised my voice, I'm sorry." My chest aches with a sadness I know goes back to the way my parents fought. They screamed at each other; that's how they spoke to one another. And that night, I know I yelled at her when I saw she was just fine and hiding in her parents' apartment. "You scared me, Soph. I thought something bad had happened to you," I tell her with sincerity I know she can hear. I know she can feel it.

"Well, you scare me, so we're even." Her voice is small, and it wavers as her eyes turn glossy.

"How? What did I do?" I nearly choke on my next words as I say, "I didn't know about your parents." My throat's so damn tight. "If I had known--"

"You would have been gentler with me?" Sophie's teeth dig into her bottom lip as she reaches up, putting both of her hands on my desk to lean forward. "My problem isn't how you treat me when I'm with you, Madox. It's that when I'm not with you, that's fine to you too. You don't mind either way."

"Bullshit." The word comes out of me easily. "If I didn't care, this right here wouldn't hurt so fucking much."

"I told you if you wanted me to stay, to just tell me so."

"I don't remember it that way," I tell her, standing up from my desk and walking toward her. The motion closes the space between us and she stands up to face me, her ass hitting the chair now behind her, making it creak against the wooden floors as it does.

When we fight, it's fire against fire. And I can see the sparks in her eyes. The venom in her voice is nothing compared to the lust. I know she still wants me. I can hear it and see it when she fights. She wouldn't be hurting if she didn't love me.

Please, just love me.

"The way I remember it is you telling me that you were worth more." It's hard to push out those words, because she was. She was worth everything; I just failed to prove it to her. Over and over again I failed. In a world where I can buy anything, I have nothing without her. None of it means anything without her. How can she not know that? "And then the next thing I heard, you'd flown across the country with Brett's sister because your parents died. That's more than a little something that may have helped me understand what you needed."

Although her face crumples, she keeps her composure steady in her voice.

"I texted you the next morning before I left. I said if you wanted me to stay, then tell me that."

Bullshit is on the tip of my tongue again, but there's a look in Soph's eyes I don't see often. Pure pain and agony. There are times to push, and times to fight. That morning she left, I didn't hear a single word from her. I know that. It's a fucking fact. She never messaged me.

"If I'd seen that message, I would have told your ass to stay where you were." I tell her the raw truth in a way I hope she doesn't fight.

"You saw it, Madox. I know you saw it and you didn't answer me, because you didn't care if I left. You assumed I'd come back. You may regret it now, but you can't change the past." Her voice is firm, just like her resolve to leave me again. I already know that's what she's doing, and I don't know how I can hold on to her. I can never hold on to her.

"There was no fucking text message. You left because that's what you do." Before the words even leave my mouth, I already regret them. They're harsh and brutal, and they spill from me out of hurt and the desire to hurt her back. "You leave people. That's what your mother taught you to do."

Regret. It's instant regret.

"I don't mean to hurt you." I barely get the words out and then shove the next sentence out as fast as I can, "I don't want to hurt you. I don't want you to run away anymore."

The mere inches separating us are both hot and cold. And as I reach out for her, she steps back.

Don't leave me.

"You're right," she says in a strained voice as she nods.

Don't leave me.

"I do always run. And that's why this has to stop."

Don't leave me.

"You told me to tell you to stay, so stay," my voice begs her. I have to grip the chair from grabbing on to her, from physically keeping her from leaving.

"I asked for time." Her eyes shine with unshed tears as she tells me, "I didn't want to fight, Madox."

I bite my tongue, holding in the bitter comment that I've given her three years. I would rather fight than watch her walk away again.

"Don't leave me," I tell her just barely above a whisper and that's when she cries, "I'm sorry, Madox. I need to be okay on my own."

I want to tell her that she is. That I'm the one who's not okay. But I can't. I can't do anything but stand there gripping the chair as she cries harder when I say nothing. And then she leaves me. I watch her leave this time, and I hate myself.

I hate the person I am. I hate that I can't show her I'm the one who's not okay.

I'm the one who needs her to stay.

Chapter 14

Sophie
Three Years Ago

Is it supposed to feel like this? This empty gnawing sensation inside that eats you alive? It was never like this before. I would leave and feel his absence but somewhere I knew he was still waiting for me. I keep staring at my phone waiting for him to text me, but he doesn't. The last text is the one I sent him.

He's so used to ordering me around, but he can't tell me to stay. I gave him an out and he took it.

I hate myself for leaving. I hate that I'm crying on the mattress that's on the floor. I hate that I'm this person. This person who needs him and runs to him whenever I'm feeling weak.

I'll learn to stand on my own. I'll learn. I just didn't think it was supposed to hurt like this. It hurts too much to be away from him.

Today

I hate myself. I hate how weak I am. I felt so strong and put together when I was far away from here, at least the last two years I did. I fooled myself into thinking I knew who I was and that I could stand on my own.

But here I am, crying in my car before a work dinner because I walked away from the man I love. He's right that I run. I'm still running. This time, I'm not hoping he'll catch me. I don't deserve it.

I'm worried I don't know how to be in a relationship without fighting. I'm worried I don't know how not to run away from my problems. I'm worried if I don't go back to Madox immediately, he'll stop loving me. And I desperately want to hear him say those words to me, to see him when he says it, to kiss him when he says it. I'm just afraid. I'm so fucking weak for this man, but I don't want to be. I just want to love him and be loved by him. I wish I were his equal, but I never will be.

One more deep breath and I touch up the concealer under my eyes, using the rearview mirror before heading into the restaurant.

It's the same place Madox took me to two days ago. I'm really starting to hate fate. She thinks she's so fucking funny.

Another deep breath, and I put on a bit of mascara.

One last deep breath, and I climb out of my car. There's a bite in the air so I pick up my pace, trying not to think about Madox and forcing a smile as the doorman lets me in to the restaurant.

"I'm meeting a party; I believe it's under Adrienne Hart?"

"Ah, yes," the maître d' says and smiles brightly, graciously not saying anything about how I bumped into him two days ago when I walked out of those front doors crying. "Right this way." He's all politeness as he walks me back to a private room.

I expect the table to be large, but it's not.

My pace slows, as does my heartbeat when I see the two of them waiting.

Adrienne, with pearls and a simple black dress. Her head held high as she talks to the man next to her.

Although it's the back of his head, I already know it's Madox. By the way he holds himself, it's more than obvious to me. I can hear the timbre in his voice when he says something.

Oh my fucking God. I can't breathe.

My mouth dries as I'm ushered to the third chair at the table and I keep my gaze on Adrienne.

Don't freak out. I breathe in and out slowly. Anger slowly drips into my blood. He better not have interfered with my work. Please, for fuck's sake. I will murder him.

My throat is tight when I take my seat. I'm stiff and my body is ice cold as I avoid Madox's prying gaze. I can feel his eyes on me, but I can't even look at him.

"Sophie dear, I'm so happy you could make it tonight," Adrienne says sweetly, like there's nothing wrong in the least, and I force my lips into a tight smile. My gaze flicks to Madox. My heart beats once.

His gaze is narrowed, his forehead creased.

My heart beats even harder, even heavier.

"I'd like you to meet my son," she says although her voice barely registers.

My heart beats a third time.

This can't be real.

Please, no. Her son?

My tight smile falters when I look at him. I don't know what to do or say, but all I can think is that he set this up.

That I didn't earn my job. That I didn't get here because I deserved it. That I was a fool to think I'd finally made it on my own.

Suddenly, my lips feel dry, and I lick the bottom one as Madox tears his gaze from me to face his mother. "Madox, this lovely lady is Sophie. She's recently been hired by the company I bought a while back that I told you about. The design and branding firm, do you recall?"

With a racing pulse, I look between the two of them. *Does he not know?*

My head is spinning, and I'm lost in a blur of questions.

"Madox," I say his name and I try to keep it polite, but still it comes out like a question, his name is uttered like a plea.

"I already know Sophie, mother," Madox informs Adrienne in a tone that's far less than pleasant, and instantly I look down to the table, feeling smaller by the second.

"What are you doing?" Madox's voice is hard. At first I think his question is for me and I'm ready to lay into him and defend myself, but it's not.

"What do you mean?" His mother's voice is an octave higher than I've heard before. *The voice of a liar.*

"I don't have time for this. What. Did. You. Do?" His voice is harder; firmer, with no forgiveness. It's nearly cruel.

I've never seen his mother or seen them together. It's nauseating to watch. There is absolutely no love between them. In the four years we were together, Madox spent every day avoiding her. I didn't feel bad for her because she never seemed to want to be with him, but right now, I feel dreadful for all of us.

"Madox, please." She merely admonishes him with disgust in her voice.

Slowly I find my own backbone, looking between the two of them and still feeling sick to my stomach. Of course the waiter would come over the second I start to speak.

"We're not interested at the moment," I bite out, and then feel awful for snapping at the innocent man. "I'm sorry," I'm quick to add. "We just need a minute." As soon as the waiter's back is turned, I look back between the two of them. Madox looks nothing like her, but he'd always told me he was his father's son.

"I deserve an explanation," I tell them, and my voice is

hard but just. "What the hell is going on?"

"Nothing." Adrienne is the first to speak, raising both of her hands and feigning innocence. "I had no idea the two of you knew each other. I simply wanted you two to meet."

Madox considers his mother for all of a second before turning his attention to me.

"I'm sorry," he tells me. "I had no idea my mother brought you here."

Brought me here.

Fuck.

Fuck.

I was right. I didn't earn my position. She knew who I was. She did this for him.

His mother starts to talk, but even I know there's no way this is a coincidence.

Madox's patience is nowhere in sight. "Just tell the truth for once in your fucking life."

"Don't speak to me like that," his mother hisses.

The tension at the table is palpable.

"I think he feels betrayed," I speak up, feeling an ache in my heart, a hole that grows larger with every second. "Just as I do, and I can't figure out why you would do such a thing. I'm not angry at you for putting me into this very," I make sure I lean forward and emphasize the next word, "uncomfortable position." I have to swallow and when I do, both of them try to speak but I cut them off. "I am not finished."

Silence. The entire room is silent.

"Madox is a good man," I start to say, looking Adrienne in her eyes, noting how she still holds herself prim and proper as I continue, "to his core. And it's obvious you've set this entire reunion up." I glance at Madox, gauging his expression. If he knew, I'll be crushed. Truly crushed that he would set me up to think I landed my dream job on my own.

"I feel used," I say and hate that the emotion comes through, "and I don't know why you think it's okay to lie." Swallowing thickly, I feel the need to add, "Your son is the best thing that ever happened to me. He is genuine and kind, and he doesn't deserve to be lied to. And neither do I."

Putting my hands up in defense I add, "I know there's a lot between you two, but if you were more sincere, Adrienne, I know things wouldn't be as bad as they are. And I certainly don't have to sit here and be a spectator to this."

I don't know how they got this way. I don't know the details. But I do know I don't deserve to sit here and feel this fucking uncomfortable.

"I have to go," I announce. Taking a deep breath, I look Adrienne in the eyes and say, "I can't work for you any longer. I'm sorry." As soon as the words have left me, it stings.

Goodbye, dream job.

Goodbye, New York.

My gaze shifts to Madox, who still looks nothing but pissed. "Goodbye, Madox," I whisper.

Chapter 15

Madox

"I don't understand what the hell you did." I say the words as calmly as I can manage to my mother, feeling a wave of betrayal but also something else. She brought Sophie here? She knew about her?

"Madox, please." My mother's voice is tinged with agony and it makes me pause after I stand up, ready to leave her.

"I promise you, if I did anything-"

"If?" The word comes out harder than I intend, and she flinches. She brought Sophie here. She brought her back to me. I can't hold on to the anger, knowing my mother brought Sophie back to me. Regardless of what her reasoning was, so long as I can catch her and keep her from running off again.

My mother's hesitant to reach out and take my hand. I can't remember the last time she's touched me other than the polite hugs we exchange in public when I agree to see her. "I just want a chance..."

"To what?" I ask her, the words pushed through my teeth. "To lie? To pretend like you did nothing?" My words turn harder, and the memories come flooding back. She didn't even cry at his funeral. Behind closed doors she didn't mind being real with my father. And the real version of her is a person I want nothing to do with.

"I have to go get her," I tell her before I can go back to what used to be.

My mother doesn't let go of my hand, although she still hasn't stood up.

"I can explain, Madox." My mother's words are hushed as she leans across the table, her forehead marred with a deep crease while worry is etched into her eyes. "Please, I can make this right, I just need to speak with Sophie."

I don't even dignify her request with a response. I've already waited too long, knowing Sophie. If I wait any longer, I may never see her again.

Just the thought of her hiding away until she can leave sends a visceral response through my chest. My pace quickens, my body fighting the urge to run.

"Madox, please, I'm trying to help!" My mother's cry carries through the restaurant as I leave the private room, doors swinging behind me.

By the time I've exited the front doors, I spot her by her car, and then I do run. I run as quickly as I can, stepping out in front of a car pulling in for valet parking. My palm hits the hood of their car, only a few feet away as they slam on the brakes.

Shit.

They stop in time, but I don't bother waiting to apologize.

"Are you okay?" the doorman asks and calls out, "Sir!" but I don't respond. They don't matter. So long as I can run to her, that's all that matters.

Two rows up, Sophie's staring over her shoulder at me, the car door open and the breeze blowing her hair behind her.

Don't run from me, Sophie, I pray as I stare straight ahead at her, moving even faster, ignoring another beep of a horn and a couple I brush past to get to her more quickly.

"Sophie!" I call out to her in the crisp night air. My lungs burn from the chill and exertion. Surprise flashes in her eyes and I can see her swallow; I can see the pain lingering in her bright blue eyes.

"Madox." She says my name reverently as she closes her door, not getting in and turning to face me instead. Her arms wrap around herself and she takes two steps toward me by the time I stop in front of her.

"Don't leave." The words slip from me before I can say anything else, and I take her arms in my hands, staring into her doe eyes. "Don't leave."

My heart pumps hot blood, hard and fast. My body is ringing and my mind screaming, *it's now or never.*

"Did you know?" she asks me quietly, and it takes me a second to realize she's referring to my mother and the shit she pulled.

"I still don't understand what the hell you were doing there."

"You didn't know?" she continues to question as if I would lie to her.

"I had no fucking idea you knew my mother, let alone that she hired you."

She considers me for a moment and then nods her head, looking as if she's going to turn around and get back in her car she tells me, "That's all I needed to know."

"I want you to stay. You told me to tell you; here I am." My voice raises when she doesn't answer me. "I would do anything to keep you. Stay with me. Whatever happened in there doesn't matter. None of it matters."

I watch as she swallows and then takes a half step closer to me. "It mattered to me," she says softly. Her lips part but she doesn't speak, looking back at the doors to the restaurant. "I thought..."

"I know. I know, Soph. I don't know why my mother does the shit she does, but I understand if you're feeling low right now." I try to phrase my next words the right way, but I don't know how to say what I'm feeling. I just want to be her person. I want her to let me love her.

"I don't want to fight, Madox," she says weakly, wrapping her arms tighter around herself and it's then that I note how cold it is. Instinctively, I try to take off my jacket, but I'm not wearing it. Fuck. I left it back in the restaurant.

Can nothing go right when it comes to us? I can't even give her my jacket when she's obviously freezing.

"Let's go back inside. We don't have to fight."

"We always end up fighting, and I feel like--"

"The reasons we fought back then... it wasn't dumb shit, Soph. We both went through rough shit and we were there for each other, but we were hurting." I nearly swallow my next words, but she still looks like she's going to run. "I hurt worse without you. I'm hurting now. I'm asking you to stay because I need you. I'm not okay. Sophie, I'm asking you to stay because I need you. Stay with me. Please."

Her baby blue eyes widen as she looks up at me, clinging to my words.

"I realized something about myself. The way I handled things back then... When you walked away, there were things I could have said. Words that would have made you stay, because you needed to hear them. I hope I'm saying the right ones now. I don't want you to leave here without me. I don't want you to walk away without knowing I want you and I love you, and whatever shit my mother is doing, I don't care about it or her. I just want you."

"Madox," she pleads with me as she wipes her eyes and I

don't know what the wretched sound is pleading for. It's hard to swallow, but it's harder to swallow unspoken words and know she may never give me another chance to speak them.

"I was afraid to talk to you back then. I was scared I'd say the wrong thing and you'd leave me, and I'd never see you again. Now I'm afraid even if I do say the right words, you're still going to leave me because it's too late."

"Madox, I never knew you were scared... You were never anything but strong." Her voice hitches on the last word as she repeats, "I didn't know," and she covers her face with both of her hands as her shoulders hunch over. The first sob is soft, but the second is harder, louder, wracking every piece of her.

"Come here," I say and pull her in close, holding her as tight as I can as she wraps her arms around me. Her fingers dig into me, clinging to me. Everyone could be watching us right now and I wouldn't give two shits. I just don't want her to leave me.

Please, don't leave me.

"Tell me if I didn't say the right things." I rock her gently as I speak; her hair brushes against my lips. "I've never done this before," I whisper, being open with my insecurity.

"I just wanted," she starts to say, and her words are strangled as tears leak freely from the corners of her eyes. She peers into mine, searching for something and I hope she finds exactly what she's looking for.

"Madox, the problem—my problem—is that I don't see

what value I could possibly bring to you." I can hear her heart beat harder, feeling it thump against my chest. "I've only ever been a burden." As the shock of her words hit me, tears stream down her face.

"Sophie--"

"No, let me, please. Please let me finish." The tips of her fingers touch my lips as she softly says, "Please."

The very real fear of her leaving me right now because she doesn't think she's worthy destroys me; I can't move an inch while I wait for her to finish.

"I don't see how I'm deserving of you. We were never on equal ground, and I could never give you anything in return like what you gave me."

Time slows, and everything blurs around her. How could she think she was undeserving? How is that even possible?

"I don't have words to describe it. You're everything to me. And I don't know how you don't see it."

"But why?" She's brushing at the tears. "How could you care for me like you do?"

"Soph, every word you've just told me, every single word, I could say right back to you. I love you, Sophie Miller, and all I want from you is to feel the same way about me."

I've never liked the look of her crying; in fact, I hated it, but right now, looking at me with her eyes glossed over and my words sinking in, she's never looked so beautiful.

"I love you." The words slip from her with the sincerity I

know they hold. She would never have to utter them again in my lifetime, and I'd still know it. I've always loved her for it, and I always will.

As she leans forward, the sound of footsteps approaching from behind steal my attention.

"Sophie," my mother's voice breaks the moment but before I can say anything at all, Sophie asks me to give her and my mother a moment.

"Only if you promise me you won't run." But even as I say the words, there's a calmness between us, one I've never felt before with her. One I hope I can hold on to until the day I die.

"I promise, Madox. I don't want to run from you. I promise. I don't want either of us to be alone."

Chapter 16

Sophie

"Maybe we should go inside." Adrienne's voice is calm as her fingers twine together and she glances around the parking lot. Night fell in the last hour and it's dark back here, save for the lampposts.

"Wait for me?" I ask Madox, and he's already nodding.

"I'll be just outside the room." His words are soft for me, but his gaze is stern and directed at his mother, who simply pretends he isn't looking at her at all.

The chill in the air nips up my arms and I nod once in agreement. I can't stand to look her in the eyes. My head is spinning, and the notion that I was only a pawn and didn't deserve my job is screaming in my head. I knew better. I knew better than to think I was worthy of a job like that.

Walking in unison, our heels click on the pavement as I gather my composure. With every step I remind myself of what just happened. He said he loves me.

Madox Reed loves me. That's all that matters.

There is no doubt in my mind. Swallowing the lump in my throat and bracing myself for what's to come, I hold on to that. It doesn't matter what Adrienne says or what she thought she would accomplish with her duplicity. Madox loves me.

Fuck, more tears gather in the corner of my eyes as I follow Adrienne to a private table in the back. I don't miss how she asks for the waiter to leave us alone for a moment. It's the same fucking room I was in two days ago. Everyone here must think I'm a fucking lunatic for constantly crying.

I couldn't give two shits what they think. Madox Reed loves me.

"I want to tell you a story, Sophie, if you'll let me."

All I can do as I sit across from this woman, a woman who has lied to and deceived both me and the man I love, is nod. I can't be angry at her, not after what just happened with Madox. But it feels like she's stolen from me.

"Years ago, as I'm sure Madox has told you, my late husband made a horrible business deal. My parents never thought the man I married was a good choice because he didn't come from money, but I knew he loved me and that was all that mattered."

Her next words are torn from her throat, barely spoken as tears gather in her eyes. "I cared for him, but when he lost so much money, Sophie, I don't know how he could have been so stupid. And that's what I told him. I was cruel and angry and bitter. My mother always told me to marry someone who loves you just a little bit more than you love him. And I thought I had.

"I still loved him, God did I love him, but we were going through very hard times and I told him I didn't. And worse. I said a lot of even worse things to him." Licking her lower lip, she focuses on something on the wall behind me, maintaining her poise although tears leak from her eyes. "I won't deny the things I said to him that last night were cruel."

Madox never told me any of this. I know he blames his mother, but I never knew they'd fought like that. That she screamed at him.

"I deserve to be alone for what I said to him. I drove him to feel unloved and unworthy. I told him..." She closes her eyes and doesn't finish. When she opens them she shakes her head and says, "Madox heard what I said, and I can't even voice it now. I can't take the words back, but I won't ever say them again. My husband wasn't well, and he killed himself that night. He was the love of my life. I regret everything that night."

"I'm so sorry," I whisper and it's then I feel my own tears.

She cuts me off before "sorry" is even spoken, waving her hand. "I'm not finished. Please, let me finish."

"I lost my husband, my wealth, and I was losing my son. He was angry, he hated me and blamed me. Madox needed to act like the man he was meant to be. He was too much like his father, that's what I'd told him when he would act out. I thought hard love was the best way to raise him. It's how my parents raised me. I was ... wrong. I was very wrong.

"Over the years, I lost him bit by bit and I didn't realize it. After Charles died, I needed my son back. I needed myself back. I was so lonely, and I hated myself for it. But Madox didn't want anything to do with me. I know he blames me, and he doesn't forgive me. I understand that, because I can't forgive myself either.

"It's only gotten worse over the years, but there was one moment, one morning where I did something, and immediately after Madox changed entirely. He became ... a shell of a man. That was three years ago, Sophie. I think you know what I'm referring to."

A chill flows through my body and the hairs at the back of my neck stand up. Wiping away the tears from under her eyes, Adrienne composes herself as she speaks.

"When this branding and design company came to me with a proposition to back them a few months ago, I knew it was a good investment to make. They had one condition that caught my eye. They wanted a new hire, one of four potential people. And your name was listed."

My body trembles as I try to stay focused. That day three

years ago. What did she do?

"You earned your position, dear, I promise you that. Your name was at the top of the short list, but I made sure they hired you. I wanted you because I knew your name. I had it etched into my memory." It takes everything in me to stay calm as she tells me what she did. It changed my life forever.

"Three years ago, I wanted my son to talk to me. To sit down at the same table as me. I wanted him to know that I loved him, and to care about me in return. But he didn't. He never wanted to see me. I went to his room and he wasn't there, but his phone was. And on his phone was a message from a girl he must have been dating."

"Oh my God," the words slip from me without conscious consent. An excruciating pain tears through me. I spent years thinking Madox didn't care. I would have sworn on the Bible that he'd seen it.

He never answered me, because he never saw the text. It was her. His mother. I struggle to breathe as Adrienne continues.

"I deleted the message without thinking twice, but I didn't see the name it was from until after it was gone. I knew your name from that list and I had it memorized because I had to look up the number that belonged to that contact from his phone. He only put, 'love her' as your name, Sophie. My son loved you, and I was willing to sweep you aside so I could have him back."

"You... you have no idea what that did to me." It's hard to contain every emotion running through me.

"I knew I'd made a mistake, and I didn't want him to hate me any more than he already did. I spent years trying to figure out how to make it right, Sophie." There's a note of entitlement in her voice, a strength that she isn't to blame for everything. And she's not. If Madox and I could have had a fucking conversation back then, a true meaningful one, the last three years could have been different.

I tried. In the last moments I had here, I tried.

And she stole it from me.

It never occurred to me how much I needed him back then. I didn't let myself think about it because I thought he truly didn't care if I'd stayed or left.

"I didn't know. I swear I didn't know how much you two loved each other. I'm sorry. All I'm doing now is begging for your forgiveness. From both of you. It took me years to realize it and even then, I didn't want it to be true. That I'd done that to my son. You left, and he was never the same. Not until now. I made a mistake. More than one, and I'm so sorry.

"Please forgive me. If I could go back, I swear I would. I'm trying to make it right." Her tone is placating at best, mostly forceful though, and I can't respond. I never thought she was my friend, she was only a woman who had given me a chance, but I still feel betrayed.

None of it matters, because I remind myself, Madox loves me.

"I forgive you, but you need to tell Madox." My voice

is eerily calm, disconnected from her pain, and it feels underserving. She's suffering; it's easy to see. But she's done this to herself, and I don't know that there's a way to get out of it. The hole she's dug is so deep.

"I just want my son to forgive me. I can't live like this. I want to love him and for him to know that I love him. I'm trying, Sophie. I promise you I will do anything to make it right."

"You need to talk to Madox, honestly. I don't think he knows you love him. And he deserves to be loved."

"I'll talk to him tonight. I'll tell him. Please, don't leave him. Please? He loves you."

"I don't know what he's going to say or think, or whether or not you two will be all right. But I know I won't let anything come between us again. I can promise you that."

Chapter 17

Sophie

There was a knock on my door at two in the morning. I was still wide awake and waiting by my phone, waiting to hear back from Madox. He dropped me off before meeting his mother at her home, for privacy. She insisted they talk tonight and I urged him to go to her, but I didn't think about sitting here waiting on him all night.

I've never been so uncomfortable being alone. I've never wanted to go to him more than I did tonight, knowing he was talking to his mother. It's been hours.

Trish kept me company on the phone. She had no idea his mother was responsible for this whole thing. The text, the job. None of us did. I knew this apartment was too much.

She had the company not just hire me, but also pay for my traveling expenses and an apartment I shouldn't have gotten. Adrienne made sure I wouldn't say no to the job offer and to coming back to New York. She made sure there was no reason I wouldn't come back.

I let Madox in the second he knocked on the door and it's been nearly an hour since then, both of us just lying in bed, staring at the ceiling and talking about it all. Every few minutes there's silence, but there's so much to talk about that the silence doesn't last for long.

"She said she'll give the company over to someone else if you'd prefer for her not to be there anymore," Madox says and squeezes my hand.

"I don't know how I feel about it all," I whisper.

"You were on their list, Soph. They wanted you."

"They're going to find out. Everyone I work for is going to find out I was basically gifted my job." That part hurts. It fucking hurts. "I love this job, and it's a big deal to me."

"Give it a week," Madox says calmly. "No one knows, and you deserve to have time to show them what you can do."

The idea of walking away from Lara Bolton and my dream job fucking kills me. I could learn so much from her. "I don't want to give it up," I tell him and he rubs his thumb along my wrist; I hope he never gives up that habit.

"Then stay, and my mother won't be involved in any way."

At his words and the harsh way they were spoken, I turn

on my side, letting his hand go and face him. Tucking my hands under the pillow, I wait for him to look at me before asking, "Do you forgive her?"

"Which part?" he asks me and I feel a swell of sadness rise up my throat. I can't even imagine how he feels. "She told my father to kill himself that night, and he did. It's hard to forgive either of them."

I watch as he swallows, his throat tightening and the small bits of stubble showing. "It doesn't feel right. I feel like telling her I'm okay with her now is the same as saying what happened that night is okay, and that feels wrong to my father. But he wronged me first."

His voice cracks and he covers his eyes with his hand for just a moment, breathing in deep. When he takes his hand away, his eyes look red, but there are no tears. "I don't know how anyone can get past it."

"I don't think anyone wants you to get past it. I think your mother just wants you to forgive her for what you can," I speak slowly, trying to keep my voice even and calm. Agony consumes me when I look at him like this. I never knew my hero was hurting. I wish when we were younger that we would have bared our souls to each other like we are now.

Everything would have been different if we weren't so scared of losing each other.

In a way, we have his mother to thank for it. I can't deny that.

Madox doesn't reply for a while and I scoot closer to him,

needing to feel my body against his.

"She brought you back to me," he says after a moment and I nod my head against his chest. Wrapping his arm around me, Madox pulls me closer. "It's hard to see her though. It's difficult to imagine being on a friendly basis with her."

"I can understand that," I whisper and he pets my hair. "You're doing really good just talking about it. You can take it day by day."

Another minute passes.

"I don't know what to say to her. I don't know what she wants from me. We were never close. I was always my father's son... which is why... fuck."

Years ago, I held him like this as he mourned his father's death. And tonight I do this same. Grief comes and goes. It's not something that's a singular notion. It's constant.

"You should talk to her," I barely speak the words. "You know I didn't get along with my mom. But I wish I'd told her I loved her before she died." My throat feels hot and my mouth dry as regret comes for me once again. "She wasn't perfect, and she hurt me with some of the things she did... but I did love her, and I regret not making sure she knew it before she died."

Madox holds me closer, tighter to him and plants a small kiss on my cheek. His touch is soothing.

"It's not my place to interfere, but she loves you and I know she has regrets. You could see a therapist, maybe," I offer, hoping he'll see someone or try to talk to her. I don't want him to live with any more regret than he already has.

I never knew how badly he hurt, and I don't want that for him. He doesn't deserve this pain.

"Can I just talk to you?" As I part my lips he adds, "And I'll listen to my mother, or I'll try to at least."

"I think that sounds like a really good plan. If you do it."

"I will."

I give him a quick kiss while holding his hands as tight as I can. "Promise me."

"I promise."

Another moment passes where it's quiet. My eyes feel heavier, my heart a tiny bit lighter, and my entire body feels warm next to him. He feels like home.

"I can't tell you how badly I've wanted this for so long."

"Talking?" I ask.

"Just being with you. It feels better when I'm with you."

I smile against his chest, but it's a mix of longing, of sadness, and of something else. Regret that we could have had this for the past three years instead of all the pain. "Yeah," I say and my voice cracks. "I know. Me too." I sniffle and refuse to cry any more before telling him, "Promise you won't stop talking to me, Madox. Even if I get upset. I just need to know you love me."

"I've always loved you. I never want to say the wrong thing."

"Madox, every word that comes from these lips is kind. You're so careful with me."

"Maybe that's why we work?" he asks jokingly, lightening the mood and I have to laugh. It's a crazy sound that erupts from my lips. As if this is what a good relationship is.

"Is that what you think? We work?" I ask him and then push myself even closer to him. Any closer and I'd be on top of him.

"Given everything we've been through, and that we still love each other, I call that working."

"That's a good point," I breathe out.

"You know I love you, right?" he asks me. I nod weakly but tell him, "I do. I know you love me."

"And is it enough?" he asks before I can tell him I love him too.

"Enough?" I question him and he tries to explain but I cut him off to say, "Madox, you are more than enough, and your love is more than enough. You are everything to me."

"So you'll stay?" he asks me and then tells me, "I want you to stay with me."

"You're crazy to think I'll ever leave you again."

"Good. If you try to run, I'm reminding you of this."

He's crazy to think I'd ever forget any of this either.

When you're young, it's easy to say it's only puppy love.

It's easy to tell yourself sweet little lies to make it all better. Or even truths, like there are so many other men out there, this one was only a phase.

But deep down I always knew I loved him in a way where nothing else could compare, and he was the only man I'd ever love. We could both feel it. We just didn't know how to show it and how to feel like we were worth being loved by each other.

It's easy to be scared by that realization, regardless of when it comes to you.

This time, I know better. That intense feeling that brings out every side of me and doesn't hide a smidgen of who I am from Madox. It's love. Pure and raw and deep. Leaving me battered and bruised.

"I love you so damn much, Madox Reed."

Epilogue

Sophie
One Year Later

"It smells so good," I practically moan as I squeeze a lime over the diced tomatoes and red onion. With a touch of cilantro, the pico de gallo is almost done.

"Just needs salt and pepper," I speak absently and then taste my part of tonight's dinner. Groaning, I let my eyes roll back and announce, "It's so fucking good."

Madox only chuckles at me. "There isn't going to be any left by the time the quesadillas are done."

"So be it," I tell him and go in for another bite.

"I love doing this with you," he says.

"I love it too, it's nice to cook together. Date nights are fun too, though," I add, slipping the spoon into my mouth and taking another bite.

"You really can't help yourself, can you?"

I pout. "You don't understand. It all tastes so freaking good."

He laughs a little harder, kissing my jaw and I steal a kiss from his lips.

"You're adorable when you're pregnant, you know that?" he says softly, lowly, and all the while looking at me in that way... the way that makes me feel like he can see everything I am inside and that he loves me still. Even the bad pieces, the parts that are jagged and don't work quite right.

I bite down on my bottom lip and take a deep breath as I ask, "About that wedding-slash-baby shower..."

"What about them?" he asks, moving his attention back to the chicken and onion mixture he's been working on.

"I don't really think we need a big wedding, so maybe we can just do something quick?" I suggest. "Just something small, same with the shower."

"For the wedding," Madox starts before I can explain myself, "it can be whatever you want it to be. And if you change your mind later, we'll have another. I want it to be whatever you want it to be." His words melt me, literally. I have to lean back against the counter.

"I was worried to tell you."

"Don't be. To tell me anything ever." He leans closer to me, giving me a kiss but he stands upright too soon. I wasn't ready for that kiss to be done.

"But I am a little worried to tell you..." Madox doesn't look at me as he talks, he only stirs the cooked onions and seasoning in the bowl instead as he continues, "that Ryan said Brett has plans for your shower–"

"Oh my God! Trish told!" I interrupt him and then cover my mouth with both hands.

"I knew it," Madox says as he slaps his hand down on the counter.

.I bite down on my lip. Neither of us was supposed to say anything to anyone. Not yet. "I couldn't help it," I say and shrug, then go back to the pico that is so fucking delicious. "She's my best friend. And *she's* the one planning the shower."

Madox grins at me. "You didn't even keep it a secret for twenty-four hours."

"What can I say?" I joke teasingly and then move to dip my spoon into a now-empty bowl... whoops. I shrug and let the metal spoon clang against the bowl as I drop it and walk back to Madox. "I'm excited. And I didn't think Trish would tell."

"Good news travels fast."

I smile against his chest as I cling on to him. "It does," I breathe out and then wonder if I should ask him what Trish asked me. I go for it, not holding back. It's one of the rules we agreed on together; we don't hold back what we're feeling or wondering anymore. It's such a simple thing, but it's made all the difference.

"Do you want to invite your mom?" I ask him and hold

my breath.

"As long as she's trying, I'm not going to keep her at a distance." Even though he answers easily, he stiffens for a moment and then walks to the sink without me.

He has a hard time talking about it, but he has ever since we got back together. Technically ever since *she* got us back together.

He washes his hands with his head down and I let him have that moment, setting the oven to 350° before walking to the other side of the kitchen where he's drying his hands and giving him a hug from behind. My cheek rests just below his shoulder, and he's quick to move his arm around me, pulling me in front of him to kiss my hair. I can feel his warm breath tickling my neck as he tells me he loves me.

"I love you too," I tell him as he rocks me back and forth just slightly. I love this man more than anything.

"It's going to be all right."

"It's going to be better than all right... if Trish is planning it. If it's Brett," I say and roll my eyes jokingly, and the kitchen fills with Madox's laugh. I love that sound.

"Oh! Real quick, I got you a gift..." I practically run to the chair in the kitchen where I dropped off my purse after work. I've been finding my place in Madox's house and redecorating it slowly. I never did before; I wouldn't have dared to presume I could. It makes me sad to think back on how I felt about myself back then. It was part of our problem. One of the many problems we had.

Regardless, this particular chair seems to be where I drop everything when I come home every day.

"It's stupid," I tell him quickly, pulling out the surprise from my purse and handing it over. "It's just a little thing... it really isn't-"

Madox reaches for the gift, letting his fingers brush against mine and shutting me up with a swift kiss. Immediately, my head feels dizzy, my heart warm and fuzzy. I think it's what being *in love* feels like.

Every day I feel it more and more, and I'm addicted to this feeling. I'm addicted to Madox and being his, and him being mine.

"If you got it for me, it's not stupid," Madox tells me and unwraps the CD. His brow furrows until he reads the title of the hit single, "I Want You to Want Me." He grins like a fool before looking up at me with his green eyes shining. "I thought it would be a parenting pamphlet or something," he tells me comically.

"You don't need that." My words make his eyes meet mine, and I'm quick to stand on my tiptoes and give him a short kiss.

"You're going to be an amazing father. I know you will."

His eyes get glossy for just a second, and he blames it on the onion that's long since been cut, which is fine, because he doesn't let me go. He keeps holding me even though I know he's thinking of his own father right now.

I don't pry, and I don't push. Every day I see more of the man Madox is, and every day I fall deeper in love with him.

"I love you, Soph," he tells me and I smile up at him, feeling everything. Every piece of us, melding together.

"I love you, too."

About the Author

Thank you so much for reading my romances. I'm just a stay at home Mom and an avid reader turned Author and I couldn't be happier.

I hope you love my books as much as I do!

More by Willow Winters
www.willowwinterswrites.com/books

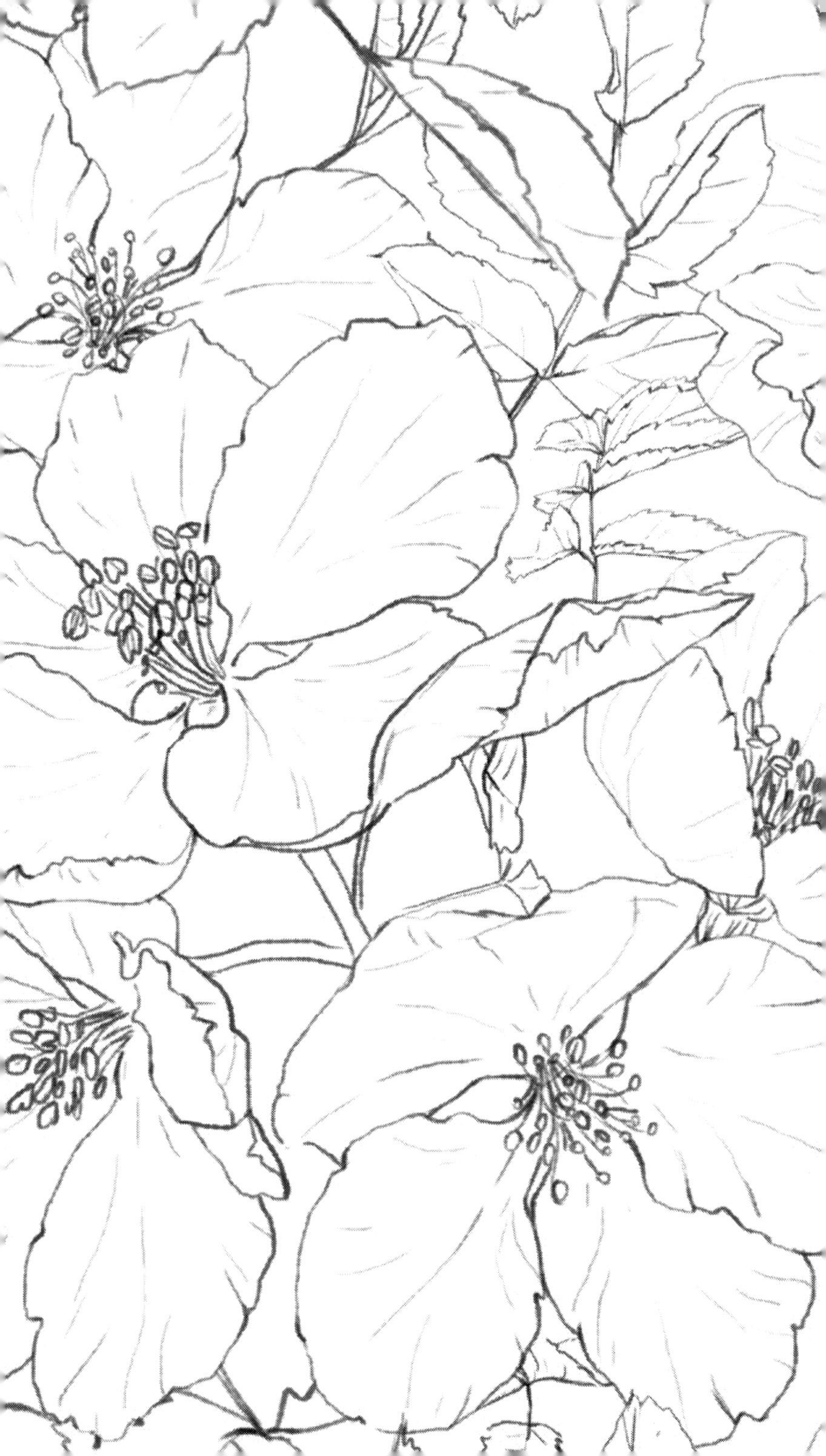